MW01039374

Tender Mercies

TENDER Mercies

KITTY THOMAS

Burlesque Press

Printed in the United States of America

ISBN-13   978-0-9832607-1-4
ISBN-10   0983260710

Wholesale orders can be placed through Ingram.

Published by Burlesque Press

Contact: burlesquepress@gmail.com

For M, who "gets me".

Acknowledgments

Thank you to the following people for their help and contributions in the making of *Tender Mercies*:

Beta Readers: Michelle, Annabel, Emma Petersen, Fallon, Claudia, Cara, & M.

Copyediting: Natasha

Cover art: Robin

Disclaimer

This is a work of fiction, and the author does not endorse or condone any behavior done to another human being without their consent. This work contains subject matter which is not appropriate for minors including depictions of abuse, slavery, dubious consent, and anal play.

PROLOGUE

"**D**arcy."

She turned at the sound of Asher's voice and smirked, wiggling her ass at him.

He sucked in a breath at the sight of her. Her long, elegant limbs, the supple leather collar, the black heels. The slutty kitty outfit he'd dressed her in, complete with a tail he'd inserted an hour before his friend had arrived. Though he wasn't sure *outfit* was the proper term, as what she was wearing was little more than black satin ribbons that crisscrossed her body, leaving exposed everything one would wish to see. Her dark mahogany hair fell forward over her eyes, giving her a look of demure submission that was so beyond the truth of his playful Darcy, it was laughable.

"Be a good kitten, and crawl over to James."

She made her way across the floor toward their guest, the bell he'd added to her collar jingling the entire way. As Asher watched from across the room, he could see the evidence of her arousal, her skin glistening with the telltale signs of her growing excitement. She loved it when James came over. Such a little exhibitionist.

James sat perfectly still, Asher's bullwhip draped across his lap. His eyes dilated, and his lips parted in a grin.

"Sir," Darcy said, bowing her head.

"You go far too easy on her, you know."

Asher shrugged. "I'm sure you intend to remedy that problem in a few moments."

It was true, he was a bit tame with her, but she knew she was his. He had the paperwork to prove it; he owned her and could do whatever he pleased. His kindness wasn't motivated by lack of right. And yet he'd been far more lenient than was probably advisable.

She'd charmed her way into his heart, and because her masochism surpassed his sadism, it was difficult to truly punish her. He'd gone so soft on her that he sometimes sang her to sleep when she asked. He couldn't bring himself to deny her anything, and now she was so spoiled that drastic measures had to be taken to correct the situation.

"James is going to punish you with the bullwhip," he said, the amusement gone from his voice. "You pushed the boundaries too far this time. For god's sake. We were in public. Smarting off to me like that? It wasn't your wisest move."

She went quiet, her delicate body still, her eyes on the floor. Her anxiety seemed to hum like a thousand buzzing bees. There was a faint tremor. She was genuinely afraid. Yes, the weight of the situation had finally landed on her. Tonight wasn't about play.

He considered calling it off, his stomach going queasy over the possibility of truly hurting her.

James caught the change in his posture. "Relax. I know what I'm doing."

"How much training have you had with that thing?" he asked, his eyes not straying from the huddled form at James's feet. Asher had practiced and practiced, but he'd never been able to bring himself to start practicing on a woman. James had.

"Enough."

"How many live human beings have you practiced on?" He looked up at his friend, still unsure of the course he'd chosen, but determined he wouldn't be the one led around on a chain.

"Five. I know what I'm doing."

"Very well."

"Master?" Darcy said.

"Yes, kitten?"

"Will you stay with me?"

He nodded, and she let out the breath she'd been holding. "After tonight I expect your behavior to change. Are we clear?"

"Yes, Master."

Asher watched grimly as James rose to his feet. The trembling in his slave had reached its zenith, and he wondered if she was milking it, trying to play on his feelings for her.

"Are you backing out?" James asked.

She looked up, the hope naked in her eyes, as if she might beg him. And if she did, he wasn't sure he'd be able to ignore her entreaty. But she remained silent, and her eyes went back down as she seemed to try to control the shaking. No, she wasn't faking it.

That knowledge made him want to stop the punishment before it began, but where would they go from here? If he showed weakness when she obviously now needed a firm hand, would either of them be satisfied again?

It had to happen.

James stood and pulled Darcy to her feet, leading her to the wall against which the St. Andrew's Cross stood. He secured her wrists and ankles to the frame so she was spread-eagled. Asher came up behind her and pulled her long hair out of the way, leaving her back exposed. She shivered.

"Do it," he said, stepping back to give James room to work.

The first snap of the whip landed perfectly across her back, eliciting a shriek unlike anything he'd heard from her before. Then the tears started coming, possibly the first real ones she'd cried in his care. His cock twitched as she pulled against the restraints, her fear and pain intoxicating. He'd forgotten this need to possess completely, for a woman to be this helpless and dependent on his kindness. The dynamic with Darcy had just never been that way. Not until now.

A few more lashes had her begging and blubbering. "Please, Master, make it stop. Please. I'm sorry."

"You've learned your lesson?"

She nodded vigorously.

He looked to James who shrugged, seemingly unconvinced that this would make much difference in the grand scheme of Darcy's misbehavior.

"One more," Asher decided aloud.

The next strike drew blood and a scream so loud it nearly busted his eardrums.

"Well, that one did it," James said.

"Indeed."

They worked together to untie her, and she collapsed in Asher's arms.

"Go to your room, and don't come out. I'll come up for you in a few hours."

"But Master, I . . . it hurts."

"I've coddled you far too long. Punishment is supposed to hurt. Things are changing between us. Go." He pointed to the staircase. Her face fell, and she winced as she hobbled across the floor and up the stairs, gripping the rail that ran along the stone wall as if for her life.

For a moment, he considered helping her, but he stayed where he was, watching her, wondering if she was exaggerating her pain now for his sympathy. Once she'd gone, he and James retired to the study for drinks.

It was late into the night when he found her sprawled on the floor in her room, asleep. So like Darcy to be a drama queen. He picked her up and moved her across the hall. She groaned in pain as he settled her under the covers with him. The groan ended his suspicions that she was just being dramatic. Maybe he shouldn't have let James go so hard on her.

He turned on the bedside lamp to inspect her back. Something looked wrong. Felt wrong. He shook her. "Darcy, look at me."

She opened her eyes with some struggle, her gaze glassy and unfocused, and the sickening thought came over him that she might not have just gone to sleep. She may have passed out from the pain. Alarm grew as he sifted through all the schooling he'd stopped using when he'd decided to ditch pre-med for business. Internal bleeding.

Possible scenarios presented themselves. Cracked rib? Punctured organ? She was so sluggish. Had she tried to come back downstairs to him? How had she even made it to her room? Had she tried to call out, and he hadn't heard her?

Her eyes drifted shut, and he shook her again. "Darcy!"

"Master . . . I'm hurt." Her hair cascaded over her back as she struggled to turn toward him, life slipping out of her more quickly now. There were a million things he wanted to say to her, a million apologies and whispered endearments. *What the hell have I done?*

"William!" he shouted, "call for an ambulance!" The servant raced into the room, already punching numbers on the phone. It was futile. Help wouldn't arrive in time; he knew enough to know that. It was far too late for gallant rescue.

He couldn't look away from her, couldn't close his eyes to her pain and the gravity of the life he'd just, in effect, taken. The life of the woman he loved.

"Master?" she whispered.

He cradled her in his arms, his thumb stroking over her cheek. His look of regret told her everything she needed to know. "Yes, baby?"

"Sing me to sleep?"

It was the last time he ever sang.

ONE

Grace Warner logged on to her instant messenger. Lucas wouldn't be on for another fifteen minutes, but he hated when she was late. *Am I really going to do this?*

From the time she'd learned of Eleu, she'd become obsessed with it. A real place where it was legal to belong to someone. The independently-governed island was kept secret, even among the kinky set. But she'd discovered it. She felt like Columbus.

How could this place exist? How could she never have known about it? At first, she'd thought her friend Lainey was just fucking with her. She'd laughed it off so as not to give away any clues of her naïveté. Privately, she dug until she found the confirmation she needed. And now she'd met a man online who actually lived there and wanted her to come to him.

Pictures had been exchanged. Naughty webcam sessions had taken place. And now he wanted her to make the choice to hand him her freedom. And the fucked-up part? She wanted to. He was rich. He was gorgeous. And he had a voice that reached inside and flipped some switch that made her want to kneel at his feet.

She wasn't uninformed about the laws of Eleu. She knew the risks. She couldn't appeal based on her rights as a citizen of any other country, because former citizenship was renounced at the gate. There wasn't even a single embassy. Tourism wasn't permitted.

No one would come rescue her, so she had to be sure. The only law pertaining to the safety of slaves in Eleu was that you couldn't kill them. If her master broke that law, that was it. Game over. Whether he was imprisoned for the offense or not, her life would still be forfeit.

She wiggled her toes—nails still wet from a fresh coat of petal pink—and looked at the clock again. Ten more minutes.

Her cell rang, and she jumped. Lucas rarely called on the phone, preferring the visual stimulation of webcam. He'd said they'd talk in instant messenger tonight; he had some work to do. She'd been disappointed but hadn't made waves about it, afraid he was getting bored with her. Tired of waiting and all her caution.

The number that lit across the screen was Lainey's.

"Hello," she said, bracing herself for more of her friend's attempts at deprogramming.

Lainey sighed over the phone.

"You just called to breathe at me?" Grace said, her eyes trained on the clock. Eight minutes.

"What do you know about this guy?" It was the question that had been asked and answered at least a hundred different times and ways, but no answer satisfied her.

"Lucas Stone. Owns an Internet company. The main focus is his social networking site. He's 38. Non-smoker. Pisces. He's got a dog, Australian shepherd. His sister is a flight attendant living in Greece. He's a Buddhist—"

Lainey interrupted the Lucas Stone resume. "No. What do you *really* know about this guy?"

"I know we've been talking online for a year, I can't find any criminal dirt on him, and he's getting bored waiting. I think if I don't go to him, he'll find someone else."

"So?"

Grace sighed. "You just don't understand."

Lainey was kinky, no doubt. But she didn't have the kind of needs Grace did. She was more about kink in the bedroom and nothing more. Her mention of Eleu had been in more of an offended feminist can-you-believe-those-psychos way than real interest. She hadn't counted on the idea lighting something inside of Grace and not fading.

"It's too dangerous. I don't care how long you've been talking or how kinky you are. You can live in a consensual 24/7 relationship here, where you'll have legal recourse if the bastard tries to really hurt you."

"Just like battered wives and abused girlfriends do? If you're with a dangerous man, laws won't protect your rights. You know that, and I know that. You either end up with a useless restraining order and a psycho that kills you anyway, or the battered wives' version of Stockholm Syndrome."

"Grace . . ."

"Safewords don't make you safe. If you're with the wrong guy playing kinky, you're fucked anyway. I've taken every precaution I know to take. I've checked out everything there is on this guy. He's squeaky clean."

"Maybe too clean," Lainey said, as if a man were evil by virtue of *not* having a criminal record.

Five minutes.

"I have to go. He's logging on in a few."

Lainey seemed as if she were going to argue, but instead disconnected the call without even a goodbye. Lainey was the only one who would fight her on this.

Grace's parents had died in a car crash, and her brother was too coked out of his mind half the time to understand what was going on in his immediate reality, let alone a thousand miles away at her house.

Another minute passed and she saw Lucas's Internet handle, *Stoneman*, flash across her screen.

Stoneman: Hey, pet. Been waiting long?

Gracie343: Only about fifteen minutes.

Stoneman: *chuckles* If only you were as eager to hop on a plane as you are to message me.

Gracie343: You know why I have to be careful.

Stoneman: I know. And you aren't wrong. A woman disappeared here. Several of us think her master killed her, but they haven't found a body.

Grace's hand trembled a little as she stared at the words on the screen. Perhaps Lainey was right. Maybe she should find some nice master at a club somewhere who would follow the laws of *safe, sane, and consensual* or be ostracized from the ranks. She shook off the paranoia. If Lucas was bad, he wouldn't be telling her about some girl that may have been murdered. It would hardly get him closer to getting her on a plane. She changed the subject.

Gracie343: You really haven't taken a slave during the time you've been talking to me?

Stoneman: Nope.

Gracie343: Why not?

Five minutes passed before the little bar on the screen lit up and dinged at her.

Stoneman: Sorry. Had to let the dog out.

Grace waited another endless minute while the text at the bottom of the chat box said: *Stoneman typing . . .*

Stoneman: It's a long process. There are occasionally sales on the island, but most men who want one do what I'm doing, find someone on the outside willing to be brought in. I know it's a big risk. I don't think I'd want a slave that agreed too quickly. It wouldn't mean as much.

Gracie343: Okay.

So maybe he hadn't found someone else. Or maybe he had. He could have a harem full of slaves and she wouldn't know until she got there. Would sharing bother her? She wasn't sure it mattered if she was willing to do this for real. And it wasn't as if she was leaving much behind. A single family member. A single friend, unless you counted co-workers, which Grace didn't. As for her career, the exciting world of retail wasn't exactly setting her world aflame. Even if it was a high-end boutique with a twenty percent employee discount. Whoop-de-do.

Stoneman: I really need to get some work done. Going to have to close out the messenger.

Gracie343: Are you mad at me?

Stoneman: No, pet. But I'm not waiting forever. This long-distance domination isn't cutting it for either of us. I want you in my bed. I'll give you another month. But if you aren't on a plane . . .

Gracie343: I know.

Stoneman: Are you going to be on that plane, Grace?

She stared at the chat box for a good three minutes. Then he logged out, perhaps tired of waiting on her answer. Maybe pissed. She didn't know. She waited another thirty minutes like a pathetic puppy to see if he'd come back. Finally, convinced he was gone for the night, she signed out of the chat client.

Seven days passed and Lucas hadn't been online. Grace had sent emails but stopped after three messages, deciding two was pathetic but three was just psycho.

He was definitely punishing her, giving her something to think about. She'd called out sick, unable to focus at work, and was currently flopped across her bed like she'd had a fit of the vapors.

A knock sounded on the door, and she wiped her eyes.

"Open up. It's me."

Lainey. Just what she didn't need. Grace lay there for another few minutes, trying not to breathe, as if her friend had suddenly developed superpowers and would be able to hear her from out in the hallway.

"I know you're in there. Mrs. Daines said you've been holed up in your apartment all day playing depressing music."

True. *Radiohead* qualified as *music to slit your wrists
to.* She knew she was being emo, but she just wanted to
wallow in it for another day or two.

"Open up or I'll go to the super. You know he'll let
me in. He thinks I've got a nice ass."

"Fucking God, just GO," Grace shouted from the
bed. She was now hanging half off, her head leaning
back, almost touching the floor.

"I'm going to get the super. I'm going to go get sexu-
ally harassed now, just for you."

Grace rolled off the bed and struggled to stand.
When she opened the door, Lainey stood there with a
smile on her face.

"Put on something that screams *submissive toy.*
We're going to the club."

Grace groaned and turned away. If it were any other
person, *the club* would mean a trendy indie band and
tossing back a few margaritas or doing body shots off
each other, if they were feeling especially frisky. But
Lainey meant the BDSM club.

"I know what you're trying to do," Grace said.

"Well, I wasn't being covert. I've got someone I want
you to meet."

"I want Lucas."

Lainey rolled her eyes and steered her by the elbow
back into her bedroom where the kinky clothes lived.
"Lucas hasn't contacted you in a week. He's done with
you. Which, in my opinion, is for the best. Eleu isn't
safe, and you know it. You don't want that life. Don't get
confused on the difference between fantasy and what's
real. It's fine to fantasize, but this isn't what you want."

"No. It's not what *you* want. Don't project." Grace
didn't have the energy for a fight, but she wasn't going
to have Lainey acting like everybody wanted and needed

the same things just because it was more convenient for her worldview.

"Eric Tatum is an investment banker. He's a respected member of the community. He's looking for a 24/7 sub. Just meet him. Talk to him. Play with him a little. See if something clicks."

Grace flopped back on the bed again as Lainey pulled out an outfit.

"Black is so overdone, but it's slimming."

"I'm a size six," Grace said, her words coming out muffled against the arm she'd dramatically thrown over her face. She was plenty slim enough and not in the mood to play kinky Halloween dress-up for a pretend master at the club.

"Just put it on. If you don't like him, I won't bother you anymore. You can go back to wallowing about how your one shot to give up all your freedom to a probable deranged lunatic on an island on the other side of the world was lost to you forever."

"I hate you," Grace said. But she took the outfit. If being a walking cliché for one night would get Lainey off her back, she'd gladly comply.

Edge was located on the far end of town in a renovated chair factory. The club had three levels meant to correlate with various membership dues. Though it was really more of a way to funnel money into the club, many of the higher-tier members considered platinum membership like some badge of true kinkiness.

The tiers were silver, gold, and platinum. Grace and Lainey were silver members, which gave them access only to the main level. Gold members got access to the main level and the second floor, and platinum members got access to everywhere including the premium dungeons. Whatever that meant.

Grace had stuffed herself into a leather corset and boy shorts. Fishnets covered her legs along with thigh-high boots. Her hair was in a high ponytail that threw a little *I Dream of Jeannie* into the look.

"I feel ridiculous."

"Well, you look great. You loved that outfit when you bought it," Lainey said.

A year ago, when I was still playing. Since Lucas and the possibility of Eleu she'd lost a lot of interest in costumes and props and protocol. It seemed all so fake. A bunch of scenes. A bunch of play actors waltzing across a stage where they competed for the *really real kink prize.*

Grace's arm went numb when Lainey squeezed it and wouldn't let go. "He's here," she breathed.

"If you're so excited, why don't you go for him?"

"Oh, I wish."

Grace turned to see a man standing in the corner that fit the tall, dark, and handsome cliché as if it had been stereotyped especially for him. He raised his shot glass and nodded before downing the drink and setting it on the counter, his eyes never leaving his prey as he moved toward them.

Last year she would have hyperventilated at the idea of a guy like that showing her even that small bit of attention, especially considering your average master didn't have the self-control to put down the corn chips and beer, judging from some of the beer guts she'd seen.

"You don't mind if I whisk her away, do you, Lainey?" Eric said when he reached them.

Grace arched a brow. "Don't I get a say in any of this?"

His eyes swept over her. "You're here aren't you? And you're dressed like you're interested."

She shrugged, already ready to go home. Lainey moved between them, linking their arms in a blatant attempt at matchmaking. "Go, Grace. Have fun. What harm is it going to do? If Lucas IMs you again, you can always go back to talking to him."

Grace's eyes widened and she looked quickly to Eric. But he just chuckled. He'd clearly been informed of the Lucas situation. She wanted the earth to open and swallow her. It was looking less like a set-up and more like an intervention by the minute.

Before she could form a reply or a good line to get her out of the club, Eric was leading her toward a set of stairs behind a gold rope.

"Where are we going?"

He simultaneously flashed his pass to both her and the bouncer. "The platinum level."

Ugh. He was one of *those.*

As if reading her mind only to find her insanely adorable, he laughed and shook his head.

The difference in the lower level and the main level was like the difference in steerage and first class on the Titanic, except in this case, the luxury was below.

The décor was plush and decadent, while still being scary as hell. The contraptions upon which both men and women were being bound and whipped were complicated and ornate. Eric took a glass of champagne off a tray and handed it to her, his shrewd eyes taking in her reactions.

"Intimidated?"

"No," she half lied. The half part was the impressiveness of the setup only. She'd tried a 24/7 relationship with all the props and protocol. It had left her cold because at the end of the day, she could leave him and go back to her former life.

Eric maneuvered her to a private booth out of the way.

"I've done the 24/7 thing before," she said when they were settled.

"Oh?" he said, not betraying any emotion on that topic one way or the other.

"It was all just a game. A big, elaborate game."

"And you want it to be real? That's why you're willing to risk everything to go to Eleu?"

Grace took a sip of the champagne, trying to hide her surprise when it turned out to be high quality. Platinum level members might not be more kinky than others, but they certainly were getting a different experience at *Edge*.

"Are you going to mock me or tell me how stupid I am?"

"Not at all. I understand completely. But are you sure you can't have that kind of bond with someone here?"

"And that someone would be you?"

"I'm looking, yes. But I'm not offering anything until I find the right person. I know at least that you're serious if you've been considering going to Eleu. Though I do think you have things a little confused."

Oh, here we go. "How so?" she asked, careful not to betray her annoyance with his paternal manner.

He leaned back in the booth, his arms crossed over his chest, a pose no doubt meant to showcase his manly masterfulness. Grace waited for the strutting peacock routine to run its course.

"I think," he said, "that reality in social situations is constructed and propped up by the group. For example, marriage is real because everyone in society agrees it is.

Ceremonies and legal marriage contracts are just a way to prop up the reality. We have the same thing in the kink world with our clubs and protocols and titles and labels. It's all just social reinforcement. But is a law really more real than a relationship? Who has the real relationship? A couple who hates each other but nevertheless are still bound by a piece of paper, or an unmarried couple with a real bond?"

An intervention was exactly what this was. She hoped he wasn't about to demonstrate why he was *real* to her on one of the pieces of expensive dungeon equipment. A spanking horse less than five feet away had just been abandoned. Grace's eyes kept drifting to it.

Eric pulled out a card and pushed it across the table. "Call me when you're ready to consider what I've said, and we'll talk further." He slid out of the booth.

"That's it?" she asked, her mouth gaping a little.

"I'm not here to win you, just to pass along a little common sense and hope it takes."

The condescension in his tone pissed her the hell off. She stood and folded the card into a tiny square. "I'm sorry you wasted your time, Mr. Tatum." She dropped it into the champagne flute and went back upstairs to the silver level.

Lainey was waiting by the gold rope like a vulture. "Well?"

"I'm going home. Don't ask me to come here again. I'm done with this fake bullshit."

Three weeks later Grace had slipped further into a funk. Work, home, frozen dinners, sleep: that was life now. She'd avoided Lainey as much as she could, not wanting to be subjected to any more of her set-ups. The truth was, if she hadn't crumpled the card and embarrassed herself by acting like a child, she might have called Eric.

If the island was no longer an option, he certainly seemed like he had it together. And in order to even *be* a platinum member of *Edge,* there couldn't be any red flags. The club was careful about that. It was one of the reasons it was considered a relatively safe place to play and meet up with potential dominants.

She couldn't bring herself to go back to the club because she was afraid she might run into Eric, probably with whoever he'd chosen to be the illustrious submissive of Mr. Investment Banker, a slap in the face she could do without. If she went back, it would be obvious she was on the prowl for a dominant, and he was off the table now—especially after that little scene the night she'd met him.

She wasn't sure what the plan was now, but her dreams of the island had grown murky and disjointed. Where once they'd been vivid and so real she could swear she was awake, now they were a passing shadow that blurred around the edges, then puffed out of existence altogether.

While she was contemplating her lack of options for a kinky future, the phrase, *Stoneman has logged in,* flashed across the bottom of her screen. For a moment she didn't breathe. He'd obviously been avoiding her, and if logged in, he'd been logging in invisibly. Or from a different account. Would he message her? Should she message him first?

The lit-up smiley face beside his name shone happily back at her while her stomach twisted in knots trying to figure out how not to fuck this up. Or even if there was a *this* to fuck up. Maybe he was just checking something on the account and then he'd be gone again, forever. Five minutes passed in limbo. Right as she was about to type something lame like *hey*, his words popped up on the screen.

Stoneman: I'll ask again. Are you getting on that plane, Grace?

She sucked in a breath and stared at the screen. He couldn't start with the easy questions.

Gracie343: I thought you were done with me. I haven't had time to think about it.

Stoneman: I call bullshit. I doubt you've thought much of anything else.

Gracie343: I didn't know it was still a decision for me to make. I haven't had the opportunity to think about it like I would have if I hadn't thought you'd abandoned me.

Stoneman: You didn't like me pressuring you. Now you don't like me leaving you in peace and *not* pressuring you. Time's up. Are you coming or not?

Gracie343: When?

Stoneman: I'll buy you a ticket for tomorrow. Planes don't land directly on Eleu, so you'll have to take a short boat trip.

Gracie343: How can I trust you when you've acted like this? You expect me to put my life in your hands now?

Stoneman: We've talked for over a year. We've sent pictures. We've been on webcam. You've been given enough information about me to verify and confirm and check for a criminal record. I've given you the tools to do that. I'm no more dangerous than any other man you could meet in a bar.

Gracie343: Except for the fact that you'd own me, and I wouldn't have any legal rights.

Stoneman: Which you've told me repeatedly that you want. Time to put your money where your mouth is. Would it be easier if you saw my face again? Do you want to talk on webcam?

Gracie343: Okay.

A few moments later she pressed *Accept* on the video call.

"Hey." His intense brown eyes drank her in. "You're dressed." He sounded disappointed.

"So are you."

He shrugged.

Though they'd played on webcam, he hadn't allowed her to use titles. No *Master* or *Sir*. Because he said it wasn't real. He only wanted a title from her if she came to the island. It had been a hard thing to get used to, and if she went to him, the complete shift in their dynamic and where the power rested would be even harder to get used to.

"I won't be an easy master," he said.

"I know."

"Do you?"

She sighed. "Are you trying to scare me off?"

"No, I just want you to know what you're getting into and come to me of your own free will. So should I buy you a plane ticket?"

"Can't I have more time? I didn't know I'd ever hear from you again."

He shook his head, his face growing stern. "Absolutely not. You've had a year. You're either in or you're out. Take the risk or stay where you are. Make a choice now, Grace."

She took a deep breath and looked around her apartment and thought of what very little she had to leave behind. Would she regret it if she said no and never spoke to him again? Or if she said yes and things went south? Everything about him had checked out. He'd admitted he wouldn't be a pushover. He'd given her plenty of time to make a choice. Hadn't he acted in good faith? She twirled a strand of hair around her fingers and finally nodded.

"Okay."

"Good girl."

Two

Eight months later, Grace had her answer. She'd regret it more if she said yes and things went south. Reality was perhaps a crueler master than Lucas, but not by much. The day she'd gotten on the plane, she'd mailed a letter to Lainey, the content of which still made her cringe:

I know you were only trying to help with Eric, but I want something real. By the time you receive this letter I'll already be on the island. I'll miss you. Maybe he'll let me instant message you sometime.

But that never happened. She'd begged and pleaded, thinking perhaps if she were good enough, he'd let her use the computer, let her contact someone from the outside world. Lainey had been right. Reality hadn't been what she'd wanted, unless it was a reality she'd orchestrated with the circumstances that turned her on. *This* did not turn her on.

She wished more than anything that she hadn't been such a brat to Eric, that she'd just tried things with him. If she had, maybe she would have fallen in love. Maybe he could have given her something that would have made her happy. Having only lived in one 24/7 relationship, she hadn't been equipped to judge them all. Eric could have been different.

This realization came far too late as she hung in the chains in Lucas's dungeon where she was beaten and violated, moving from the nightmare of being awake to the nightmares of sleep on an endless loop. As it turned out, he had no other slaves, at least not at the moment, though she desperately wished he did. Anything to cause him to turn his attention and obsession onto someone else. Anyone else.

She shuddered as she thought of her first day in Eleu.

"You understand the rights you are relinquishing and that you no longer claim citizenship in any country?" The question came from an older man with kind eyes.

Grace nodded, her stomach doing a little flip from both excitement and nerves.

"You are here of your own free will?"

"Yes."

"No one has coerced you in any way to come here?"

She thought for a minute. Had Lucas coerced her? Their last video call had seemed pretty high-pressure. Then again, he'd waited a year, showing a level of patience that had surprised her. And he'd spent a full month away. It was pretty hard to coerce someone when you weren't even talking to them. If she'd been wired any other way she would have gotten back *out there*, started looking for someone else and given up the fantasy of the island.

"Miss?"

Her gaze shot back to the customs agent and she flushed a little. "No."

His eyes seemed to delve into her soul, as if trying to determine if she spoke the truth and if she showed any signs of distress. After a few moments, he nodded and slid an official-looking piece of paper across the desk.

"Sign this and hand over all identifying cards and other similar materials that you have on you: driver's license, passport, etc."

She read the paper, knowing what it said already. Lucas had emailed her a copy of the form several months prior. Still, she read it again just to be sure. She hesitated for only a moment before scrawling her name across the bottom, making her now and forevermore subject to the laws of the island. Her hand shook a little as she slid the requested materials back across the desk.

"Are you sure?" he asked. "There are few laws that will protect you here."

"I've known him for a year."

That seemed good enough for the agent.

Once she was finished there, she was taken directly to Lucas who was waiting out back, dressed in an expensive, dark suit. His eyes practically glowed in anticipation of possessing her.

She'd goggled at the size of his house when they arrived and bent to scratch the Australian shepherd behind his ears. The dog jumped on her and licked her face.

And that was the end of normal and safety.

She was taken to the incinerator in the basement. He took the things she'd brought to the island and tossed them in. They were things that reminded her of home, things that gave her comfort.

Her hand flew to her mouth as her belongings went up in flames.

"That life is over," he said gruffly. When the tears flowed freely down her cheeks he said, "I told you I'd be a hard master. You should have listened to me and taken it seriously. Strip."

Grace felt numb. Her first instinct was to run, but even if she got out of the house, this wasn't her homeland. There was no one who would save or protect her here. She'd be a runaway slave, punished in whatever way their law dictated. There was nowhere to go.

As if a switch had flipped, she went into survival mode. The idea of happiness and contentment leeched out of her like so much petty frivolity, replaced by a need to appease him, to do whatever it took to stay alive. She hurriedly took off her clothes.

"Jewelry, too," he said.

She took out her earrings and handed them over, then looked down at the garnet ring on her hand.

"Please, not this one. It was my mother's."

He'd already tossed her clothing and earrings in the fire, and now his hand was out, waiting for the ring. "Now!" he barked. "You don't want punishment on your first day."

She struggled to get the ring off and gave it to him, closing her eyes so she wouldn't have to see it tossed in to be destroyed with everything else that held meaning to her.

"I don't understand . . . why . . . why are you being this way? You weren't like this before." She knew she sounded naïve and stupid, but she'd thought she'd been so careful, so smart about everything. But how smart was it to fly thousands of miles to give yourself over to a practical stranger to do with as he wished? Of course he would be decent online, where he had no power.

Her eyes focused on the ground, unable to look at him after she'd walked right into his trap. She jumped when he laughed.

"Sweet, little Grace. I like slaves who are careful, who agonize over the decision. You're the one I had to fight hardest to acquire. I found several potentials to replace my last slave, but they were all too stupid. After a week they were ready to come here. But you . . . you were different. You were a prize worth owning."

"What happened to the last slave?"

"Oh no, pet. You won't have an easy slip into peaceful death with me. I sold her last week. I won't be at all surprised if he kills her, though."

The tears fell silently, and she had to take slow, deep breaths to stay quiet. She didn't resist when he put her in a cold, dark cell and left her for the night.

He'd left her there three days, feeding her bland food through a slot in the door. It was as if he were sending her the message that she wasn't all that important; he wasn't so taken with her that he had to play with her right away. She was expendable and easily forgotten.

When he'd finally stepped into the room, she'd been so desperate to please him, to gain any level of favor at all to improve her situation, that she'd obeyed him without question. But nothing was ever good enough. Nothing had stopped his cruel words or his brutality. The words "good girl" hadn't passed through his lips again.

The door to the dungeon creaked open, snapping her back to the here and now. She knew it would hurt worse if she tensed, but she couldn't stop herself from holding her body rigid. If only she could just relax and let the pain wash over and pass through her.

"Have you had time to think about your mistake, pet?" *Pet.* The word was such a mockery. An endearment from before, a word that indicated some level of care and affection. And yet there was no care or affection between them. There was only sadism on his part and desperation and fear on hers.

"This slave begs forgiveness. She won't be bad again." She couldn't stop trembling in the chains. No matter how many times this happened, the terror didn't stop. She kept hoping she'd become desensitized to it, that by some miracle she could learn to hover outside her own body so that whatever damage was done couldn't touch her but would only touch the body of *that girl*, the one that wasn't really her. It would be bad enough to just watch. But if she could watch and not *be*, that would be better.

"Are you sure? I feel you should be past the point of breaking dishes when I bring you food. How do I know this isn't some rebellion on your part?"

She remained silent because it was the smart thing to do. She'd long ago learned that when in doubt, just be silent. Her master loved hearing himself speak. When he wasn't calling her *pet* or telling her she was a worthless piece of shit, he used the word *you*, as if only when he spoke to her did she have form or life. When she spoke of herself, it was always in third person, as if she were an inanimate object that could not have thoughts or feelings or needs. If she ever spoke the words *me* or *my* or *I*, the punishment was swift and severe. He'd broken her of the habit of seeing herself as a person in the first two weeks.

Even her name felt like some disincarnate thing that had long been separated from her being. *Grace. Grace. Grace. Grace.* Just a sound. An odd sound. She could barely remember what it meant. Or maybe she just didn't want to. *Grace* was like *pet*. And she could only handle being slapped with one of those words right now.

The whip came down over and over. He'd stopped speaking, more interested in hearing her screams and begging. She always begged; she couldn't help it. And it only made her more ashamed that she would give this monster anything he wanted, that she would continue to play into his hands so predictably.

She could feel the trails of blood flowing down her back when he stopped. Then he was inside her, fucking her. She couldn't bring herself to think the word *rape*, even though she knew. To heap that ugly word on top of everything else was the last little straw that would make her mind come undone.

"So wet," he growled in her ear. "You like this shit, don't you, pet?"

She shuddered as the tears fell harder. No matter what a sick fuck he was, her body still responded. Her kink had never been something she'd seen as an aberration or something that was *wrong* with her before Lucas. But now, in light of how he'd broken her, how could she see herself as anything but disgusting? Because no, she didn't *like this shit,* and yet, her body answered his as if together they were a symphony of something beautiful, the kind of something she'd hoped they could be but weren't.

Lucas gripped her throat hard enough she knew there would be a bruise. "Answer me, slave."

"Yes, Master," she gasped out. *Only because it's what he wants to hear.*

"Tell me you're mine, you worthless slut."

Tears pricked at the corners of her eyes. "This slut is yours, Master." *Only because it's what he wants to hear.* She had to hold onto that thought and repeat it in her mind so she wouldn't forget. Her body may have submitted to him, but she hadn't yet lost her mind. She prayed she could hold onto that one secret space within her. The thoughts Lucas could never know about. The thoughts of him dead and broken before her. And somehow being free of him. He always kept her locked in the dungeon when he couldn't watch her because deep down he had to know she wasn't really his.

When he was finished with her, he unlocked the chains and let her fall. "Clean yourself up. We're going out."

The sound of his boots receded, and the door slammed behind him. Normally those were the sounds that made her body unclench and allowed her to relax, but not tonight. He wasn't done with her yet.

She lay on the stone floor, catching her breath. There was a crude shower and toilet on one end of the room, as well as a sink and a cabinet that contained first aid supplies. Over the sink hung an old mirror, the one thing in the room that allowed her to witness the life slipping from her day by day. The only evidence she had that she wasn't already dead.

Showering would hurt too much. She'd have to run water in the sink and clean off the best she could. The bandage supply was running low. She'd have to ask for more soon, something she dreaded. Asking for anything only meant more suffering for whatever it was that she needed. He always made her hurt before he gave her anything. He wanted her to remember he was God. But how the fuck could she forget?

The one reprieve was that he wouldn't beat her again, at least not across her back until it healed. He'd find other punishments to torture her with instead. Things that wouldn't leave marks. Or he'd leave marks elsewhere. He didn't seem to want to kill her or physically damage her beyond repair. It was a bad sign that she wasn't sure if that was a good thing or a bad thing.

Lately Lucas had been taking her out a lot more to clubs and parties. She wasn't sure what that meant. Each time, she was afraid he'd share her with another, but so far that hadn't happened. Tonight it was a large brick building with a circular driveway. Cars were parked all the way out to the road. All black luxury sedans. It looked like the secret service was having a dinner party.

She huddled beside her master outside, nothing but a black velvet cloak and slippers to separate her from the chill in the night air. The palm trees towering overhead rustled in the breeze. Whispering about her.

The door opened and a butler took Lucas's coat and Grace's cloak and slippers. She looked down at the ground, wrapping her arms around herself. She'd never get used to being like this without clothing to shield her from strange, prying eyes. They went down a flight of stairs until they were in a large, dungeon-like room. There were many men down there—too many to count—and about five other slaves.

Lucas surveyed the room, and then picked a couch to sit on. He snapped and pointed at the floor. She knelt on the ground beside him, her breathing coming fast. Her master seemed to have a new sense of purpose lately. She wasn't sure what it meant, but each time he brought her to one of these mysterious functions, he seemed more focused.

At previous gatherings they'd stayed on the fringes, observing. Now he seemed in the thick of things, and several men came up and spoke to him. Grace couldn't follow the conversation because they were speaking in the language native to the island. Lucas had been careful to only speak English to her, obviously not wanting her to understand when he spoke to others.

She flinched and cringed away when several of them touched her. Some took her chin and forced her eyes to theirs, turning her face this way and that, running their fingers through her hair. Others stroked her breasts and between her legs. The latter action brought a chuckle. Though Grace didn't understand the language, she knew they were remarking on how aroused she was.

Each time a different male approached and started touching her, she was afraid Lucas would allow the man to borrow her. But they simply conversed with her master for awhile and then nodded and walked away.

Hours drifted by. There was dinner and drinks in a dining room, followed by more talking. No food was brought to her. She knew something important was being discussed. Was she being sold? It was the only thing that made sense in light of the business-like way the men all behaved.

She tried to think what that would mean for her. To be sold. She'd given up her silly fantasies. The reality was that she was chattel and whether it was Lucas or someone else, it was going to be bad. It was never going to be okay. The best she could hope for was to survive, though she wasn't sure survival was the best outcome anymore.

Out of the corner of her eye she glimpsed a figure standing in the doorway, a man who'd decided not to dine. Something compelled her to look up, and when she did she was met with the most brilliant blue eyes she'd ever seen, eyes that stared at her so hard she had to turn away. But it wasn't fast enough.

Lucas had seen.

He rose from his chair and jerked her to her feet. The back of his hand came across her face so hard and fast she lost her breath. Voices that had been speaking ceased as he gripped her throat and pulled her close, his mouth pressed against her ear.

"Have you taken a liking to Asher Collins?" he whispered. "He's the one I told you about last year. The one who killed his slave. Be thankful I've let you live, pet. You seem to have particularly dangerous taste in men."

He shoved her back to the floor, and conversation resumed as if this were all no big deal. Just business as usual. Just how one treated a slave. She didn't make another sound as the tears rolled down her face, so as not to call his attention again. Though she tried very hard not to, she couldn't help looking to the doorway one more time. But the man was gone.

THREE

A sher sat quietly in his study, a glass of scotch in one hand. He'd been staring at the fireplace flames for a solid hour since he'd gotten back from the showing. There had been several slaves on offer this season, and although he hadn't spoken with any of the owners, he'd hung back on the edges, observing.

It had been almost a year since he lost Darcy. *Since I killed her,* he corrected himself. It may not have been his hand that landed the fatal blow, but it was still his fault. His fault for not taking her complaints seriously and getting her help. Nothing would ever change that.

He hadn't spoken to James since they'd buried the body together. As the dirt had covered her, his friend had made some offhand remark about going to live with the natives. Asher thought he'd been kidding, but then he didn't return to his home.

Though they'd been best friends since college, doing everything together—including getting rich and coming to Eleu—after Darcy was in the ground, the cord was severed. Asher hadn't been able to bring himself to turn his friend in, but he couldn't look in his eyes or hear his voice again, either. It seemed James felt the same way.

For months Asher had stayed in, not receiving visitors. Gradually his need to possess a woman, the same need that had brought both he and James to the island, started to reassert itself. Now he was bargaining, making a list of rules and safeties so he could trust himself with another life.

He could own another woman. No, she wouldn't be his Darcy. She'd be whoever she was. Maybe he'd love her and maybe he wouldn't, but he still had needs, and right now the most powerful need he had was to move on. Perhaps atone.

One side of his mouth quirked wryly at the idea of atonement. As if anything could pay for what he'd done. The only thing that moved him forward was knowing that what happened with Darcy would never happen again because he wouldn't leave his slave unmonitored after punishment, and he would mete out all punishments himself. He would take the responsibility, as he should have to begin with.

He shut his eyes against the memory of Darcy dying in his arms. The tight feeling he got in his chest when that memory came forward had dulled only slightly in the intervening time.

Asher set the scotch on the table beside his chair and got up to pace. Sitting still was impossible when he was on the cusp of bringing a pet into the house. He'd seen the one he wanted: Lucas Stone's slave.

He'd watched from a distance, growing increasingly agitated at the way Lucas treated her and all the men who walked by to paw at her. Of course, nothing they were doing was illegal. Many had argued for anti-cruelty laws, but the policy changes always got shot down. After all, one slave's cruelty was another's happy existence. They *had* chosen this life after all. They'd known the risks. They were all questioned and psychologically assessed before being allowed to stay in Eleu, as were the men.

Lawmakers had argued that with cruelty laws, a slave would be able suddenly to appeal to someone to rescue her from this or that. Many would work the system to their advantage and end up the ones with all the control and power. Masters would fear punishing a slave as he saw fit because she might tell the authorities that she'd been cruelly tortured. And wasn't that the world in which they'd already lived? A world of choices and freedoms submissives had wanted to hand over and dominants had wanted to take? Wasn't this the utopia they'd always dreamed of, where they could each follow their own perversions without anybody else's nose in them?

He didn't entirely disagree with the current policies, but even so, there were slaves who had fallen through cracks, who were being brutalized in ways they'd never genuinely signed on for, who'd been victimized by monsters who had slipped through the psychological screenings at the gate. Lucas Stone's slave was one of those victims. Asher had seen it in her eyes.

And the fact that her back had been bandaged on the night of a showing—by her from the looks of it—was bad form. Any master who would show his property with the intent to sell right after he'd left marks wasn't fit to own another person.

He remembered when he'd lived in the States, how he'd witnessed animal cruelty, people who left dogs chained up for weeks with barely enough food or water, cats who had been left flea-bitten in crates. Why would one own a pet if they only intended to mistreat it? To Asher, slaves were the same as pets. Why acquire one if you were just going to abuse it? You could never truly own something that hated you. But some masters, like Lucas, were too fucked up to get that.

Asher moved to the wall of books and pulled a green leather volume out halfway. The bookcase slid to the side to reveal a secret passage. It wasn't *that* secret, of course. William was aware of it. He'd been quite amused by it, in fact. The island was a place where fantasies became reality: dreams of owning a slave, having a mansion, having a secret passage. Whatever he'd wanted so far in his life, once money became no object he'd been prepared to do anything to get everything on that list.

Some wealthy men bought jets, some liked to hide extra rooms in their house. He flipped a switch to turn on lights and descended the stone staircase. As nice as the idea of torches lining the walls had seemed, he'd opted for more practical dome lights that created a similar ambiance.

He remembered when Darcy had come over and how she'd squealed in delight at the secret dungeon room. She'd been fresh from a life of freedom living in Europe. Like many of the masters on the island, he hadn't wanted to buy a pre-owned slave. He'd wanted someone fresh. Someone he could mold completely as he liked from the ground up. Perhaps he'd feared he wasn't a brutal enough master, that his kindness would be seen as weakness by someone with more experience. And sometimes, perhaps it had been.

He'd allowed her to wrap herself around his little finger, showing her leniency when he should have shown her discipline. In the end, he'd lost control of her so much it had taken James and a bullwhip to right the balance. But then there had been nothing left to balance.

He crossed to one of many boxes of toys and implements of pain and dug around until he found it: the whip that had killed Darcy. The bullwhip still had a bit of her blood dried on the tip. He could no longer leave the weapon hidden away in a chest. He had to see it, every day. If he was to own another slave he had to be reminded of what his mistakes could cost him so he wouldn't make them again. He hung the coiled whip on a hook at eye level.

His mind went to the slave. He didn't even know her name yet. He'd know once he had the paperwork on her, assuming Lucas would sell to him. There were a couple of others who'd shown a great deal of interest—too much interest for Asher's taste, and their reputations weren't much better than the bastard she was with.

The longer he stood in the dungeon, the more obsessed he became with having her. She was so pale and seemingly fragile. How she'd survived under such brutality he had no idea. Her hair, like spun gold, had been long and covered a good portion of her back. But of course the edges of the bandages had shown, and when she'd turned he could see the blood that had seeped through.

Her body drew his eye, but he was ashamed to admit, it was her fear and desperation that had awakened him. His cock had jumped to attention imme- diately as he'd taken in the sight of her. She had delic- ate, pert breasts, which her master had neglected to pierce. No piercings below her waist, either.

It was an indication that he'd always intended to keep her to entertain himself for a while and then sell her for a profit. Unpierced slaves were easier to sell since most masters wanted to do that themselves. Piercings were personal, much like a brand, and not something many wanted secondhand. It would only drive the price down. Which begged the question of why he'd present her beaten like that. Such a thing was only going to appeal to the lowest common denominator—yet another hint Lucas had been genuinely mistreating the girl, not fulfilling mutual needs.

He'd broken her, possibly beyond repair, and if Asher didn't get her, it was going to be a downward spiral until one day she disappeared. He could still see her brown eyes when they'd met his blue. He imagined at one time they'd been warm and had sparkled with wicked thoughts and fantasies. Now they were just hollow. Empty.

Why are you doing this? It won't bring Darcy back.

Intellectually he knew that was true, but emotionally? He felt if he could bring this one back from the brink, if he could save her, he would balance some kind of cosmic scale. A life for a life. If he could do that, then maybe he could sleep through one night without Darcy haunting his dreams.

It wasn't the only reason he wanted the slave, of course. He didn't want another brat that would remind him of his last slave. Or someone who would be demanding. As broken as this one was, she wouldn't demand or insist on anything. She'd warm his bed and do what he asked. It would be simple. Free of complication. Maybe her presence would quiet the mess his mind had become.

He turned quickly when he heard a sound on the stairs.

"I apologize, sir. Mr. Lucas Stone is on the phone for you."

"Thank you, William."

The butler made a little bow and ascended the steps. Asher took one last look at the bullwhip and followed.

"Yes," he said, when he picked up the phone. He placed the mildest edge of irritation in his voice, knowing the son of a bitch might not sell her if he thought Asher wanted her too much.

"I see you took an interest in my slave tonight," Lucas said, getting right to the point.

Asher made a noncommittal sound. "She was all right, I suppose."

There was an amused chuckle on the other end. "You didn't make an offer for her."

"I'm just looking. Not sure I'm ready to buy."

"I can see why you might hesitate, after your last slave was deemed a *runaway*."

The way he said the word *runaway* made it clear Lucas was as aware as everyone else that she'd died, though the rumors were that it had been directly by his hand.

"Surprising that they never found her. How many places can there be to hide? Or maybe she swam off the island or escaped in a little boat."

Asher volleyed his own false speculations back. "Perhaps someone without a slave found her and took her. Even with the legalities, it can be hard for some to get their own, either because the price is more than they want to pay or because they have trouble finding someone who'll come over from elsewhere."

"I'll sell her to you for a million," Lucas said.

Asher swallowed. *Don't be too eager.* "A million in island currency or another currency?"

"Island, of course."

"Of course." A million in island currency was more expensive than a million in any other currency. He was sure the asking price was higher than the other men had offered. Not that anyone would find her worth less than that amount, but it was a high price for anyone's blood. The idea of giving a bastard like Lucas Stone that kind of money repulsed him.

"Seems high. Not sure I think any slave is worth that amount. She'd have to be very well-trained. How long have you had her?"

"Oh, she's well-trained. I've had her just over eight months. She's extremely easy to control."

"Really? What works? What is she afraid of?" Asher steeled himself for the list. If he was going to have her, he needed to know exactly what would trigger her, so he'd know what to avoid. Building trust would be hard enough after what she'd been through.

A laugh. "You sadistic bastard. I knew I picked the right buyer."

"I haven't said I'm buying," Asher corrected.

"Of course, but I think you will." Lucas's voice dripped like pond sludge over the phone. "Let's see . . . the girl has almost no pain threshold. It doesn't take much to make her scream. And yet, it all turns her on, on some level. I've never been inside a woman so wet. She's afraid of isolation, darkness, cramped spaces, bondage if you leave her alone, hunger, any of the heavier implements such as whips and canes . . ."

If she was actively terrified of all of those things, it was only because Lucas had used them to torture her.

". . . She's afraid of dogs. So if you have one, I'm just saying."

"Dogs?"

"What can I say, my puppy really likes pussy." He laughed again.

Asher's knuckles turned white as he gripped the edge of the table. Bile rose in his throat.

"Of course she *acts* afraid of dogs, but she seems to enjoy it once he gets going," Lucas continued, unaware of how much Asher wanted to kill him.

"Hmmmm. I still think a million is too high. I might offer half a million. You know that's the going rate." He held this breath, wondering if he'd pushed his feigned disinterest too far.

"Three quarters, and I'll send the paperwork over for you to sign tomorrow evening."

"Done."

He snorted with disgust as he disconnected the call. His skin crawled just thinking of that girl with Lucas for so long. When he looked up, William was standing in the doorway holding a cup of coffee, an excuse to stand there and eavesdrop.

"How much did you hear?"

He crossed the floor quickly and placed the mug of steaming liquid on Asher's desk. "Most of it. I apologize, sir."

There was a look in William's eyes that said he had a strong opinion but wasn't going to be stupid enough to share it.

"You may as well just say it."

"Well . . ." William hesitated only a moment before plowing through his prepared commentary. "If you'll excuse me for saying it, are you sure you're ready to bring a pet into the house? And one so . . . damaged?"

Asher stared hard at him, and William looked away, pretending his interest had been drawn to a vase of lilies.

"Is that all?"

"Perhaps you could take her off the island. Set her free."

William always did have such a soft spot for pets, be they animal or human. He'd worked for Asher before they came to Eleu, and it had become clearer over the years that he only barely tolerated his employer's perversions. The fact that he'd kept the secret of what had happened to Darcy that night spoke of his loyalty in the face of his distaste.

"Absolutely not," Asher said. "In the first place, she's costing me a lot of money. No way in hell am I parting with that kind of cash only to set her free. This isn't Thailand, where you pay to release birds for sport. And those birds are never truly set free, are they? They're trained to fly back to repeat the process all over again."

William looked at the floor.

"She's wired for this. As I am. If she wasn't, she wouldn't have come here. Setting her free won't change who she is. If this wasn't in her, she wouldn't have made it past the scrutiny of the customs agents—"

"—But if she's broken—"

"If she's broken, she's in far greater danger out there in the free world than she is in here with me. She'll only end up with someone else who will hurt her. She no longer has the tools to pick well, and even if she did, she'll never trust herself again. She'll get desperate and lonely someday and fall prey to another abusive asshole."

"This won't bring Darcy back."

Asher suppressed a growl. "I know that. Do you think I don't know that? I don't have any illusions I can fix her. I just need . . ." He searched for a word or sentiment he couldn't bring himself to say. Still, the word stole into his mind and bloomed into full existence in the silence of the room—*forgiveness.*

FOUR

Grace jolted awake with that awful sensation of falling, triggered by the door slamming against the wall. A bit of light spilled into the dungeon, and she huddled farther into the corner, trying to disappear. Sometimes she fantasized about shrinking down so tiny he couldn't see her, then hiding in the crevices between the stones.

He'd given her a tattered mat to sleep on and one old blanket with holes the dog had chewed into it. She squeezed her eyes shut tighter, trying not to think about the dog. Though Lucas slept in a warm, opulent room that stood as the crown jewel in a warm, opulent home, he kept her underground like some dirty little secret: cold, without clothing, barely fed.

He flipped a switch and the naked bulb overhead snapped to attention. Opening her eyes, she could see the barest smirk playing across his lips. "Good morning, pet. Did you dream about me?"

Dreamed about stabbing you to death, she thought. But she'd never be brave enough to say something like that. He reached outside the door for the tray of food he'd brought down with him. Scraps from last night's meal. He hadn't even brought her water. She'd have to drink it from the sink. She wasn't sure how much longer she could go on like this, surviving on almost nothing while Lucas used her for his amusement.

He put the food on the ground between them and crouched down next to her, a thoughtful expression on his face. "We are at an impasse."

She looked up from the plate, dreading whatever might be coming next. She tried not to cringe when he ran his hands over her.

"I can't finish you. No matter what I do, you hold onto something that I can't touch. And I refuse to be bested in that way by chattel."

For a moment, Grace's life scrolled through her head as if she were trying to hold onto the good memories from before Eleu, because it felt as if something very important were happening. Like something big was ending. The words Lucas spoke were laced with finality. She thought back to the night before, to that house and those men, and the talking in the language she hadn't been taught.

"I've sold you to a harder master. If he doesn't break you, he might just end you, like his last slave." Lucas barked out the name, "Asher," and then the man from the party was filling the doorway to the point where he blocked out all the light from outside the room.

Close up, it was obvious he was a good six inches taller than Lucas. Broader, too. Grace's eyes drifted to large, strong hands. Hands that could crush her. Then she looked up into the angriest eyes she'd ever seen.

She shook her head. "No, please, no." Maybe death was better than this life, but faced with the reality of a known killer standing there ready to take her home with him, she couldn't stop the panic from overflowing. "Master, please. Don't do this. Don't sell this slave. She'll change. She'll be better."

"It's too late. He's already paid me." Lucas stood and moved against the wall. Now nothing blocked the path

between her and the large, intimidating presence blocking the exit.

Asher took a few steps into the room, and she moved
back into the corner, as if her retreat would impede him
or slow him down. He reached down and gripped her
firmly around one arm, hauling her up to stand. She
struggled in his grasp, her brain suddenly stuck in a
loop. *This is the man who is going to kill me.* She'd
always believed that eventually she'd die at Lucas's
hands, but now she knew otherwise.

"Do. Not. Fight me," he snarled.

She froze at the ferocity of those words, her eyes
raising to his. Everything stopped for a moment, and
she spent a timeless eternity drowning in his eyes. Some
wild part of her felt he was trying to communicate in
another way beyond words, but she was too scared to
hold onto the thought long enough to take it apart and
analyze it.

When he guided her out of the room, she didn't give
him further trouble.

At the front door, he draped a cloak around her and
led her outside. She had to blink and squint against the
sunlight. Birds chirped in the distance, bathing the day
in happiness she knew she'd never feel again.

Though Lucas had taken her out some in the time
he'd had her, it had always been at night, to parties and
clubs, to show her off, or, more recently, to arrange her
sale. The day she'd first walked into his home had been
the last she'd seen the sun—until now.

Asher pulled her into the backseat with him, and the
driver started the car. She avoided his eyes, too afraid to
see that fierce anger blazing behind them, an emotion
more intense than she'd ever gotten from Lucas.

Her former master had been a great mimic of
humanity when he'd only had to be behind a webcam,

but the truth was clear once she'd stepped into his house. He was empty inside. Asher was the opposite of empty. That kind of intensity ignited new fears. What was a man with that kind of emotion capable of? How easy would it be to set him off, and what would be the consequences when she did?

She looked out the window, watching the trees go by in a blur. Grace hoped the trip wouldn't take long, but also that it would take forever. Both conflicting thoughts she held in her head with equal fervor. If it was a short drive, this uncomfortable feeling of being so close to him in an enclosed space in uncertainty could end. If the drive was long, whatever fresh hell was waiting for her on the other side of the trip would be delayed.

He finally broke the silence. "Pet?"

Grace recoiled at the endearment, but forced herself to look at him. He appeared disappointed. Buyer's remorse? Her long hair had shielded the marks on her back from his eyes, but soon enough he'd see them and realize they weren't just fresh lashes that would heal and be erased, but scars, too. Things that marked her as far from perfect. If he'd spent much money to acquire her, she was terrified of what would happen when he saw them.

"You don't like that name, do you?"

She remained quiet because it didn't seem there was an answer that would please him. If she said she liked it fine, he would think she was giving him attitude. If she said she didn't like it, well, wasn't that more of the same? It felt rhetorical anyway. Instead, she watched him and waited for whatever came next.

He seemed to be debating something in his head, a fight that went on for quite some time. She held her breath throughout the internal struggle. Finally he sighed and said, "How about kitten?"

Stunned silence followed, and suddenly she was aware of just how unprepared she was for living with another master on the island. Lucas had never given her any standard protocol to follow, and she had no idea how to speak to this new variable. She looked at the trees again. She was aware that she was crunched up against the window with a good foot of space between her and her new master.

He chuckled. "Well, I know you speak." Since they'd gotten into the car, his voice had remained gentle. Nothing like what she'd experienced in the dungeon when he'd warned her against struggling. A part of her wanted to believe in this, that the sunshine and birds all somehow forecasted a bright new beginning, the kind of life she'd thought she was getting when she came to Eleu. But believing and then falling so far again . . . Hope wasn't worth the price.

Then his warm hand was in hers, and he was pulling her close against him. He smelled like spices, rich and dark. Her ear pressed against the middle of his chest, and she could hear the steady rhythm of his heartbeat. Grace couldn't help tensing, afraid that after having been in the dungeon she was messing up his suit. She worried she'd be punished for it. Perhaps he wanted to lower her guard so he could hurt her more.

Lucas had done that for the first ten minutes as they'd stood in the entryway. He'd let her take in the extensiveness of his wealth, let her hope for one moment that somehow she'd share in all of that, that she'd be his pampered pet. And then they'd gone to the basement with the cell that was to be her home.

On occasion, he'd taken her upstairs, mainly to his bedroom, but she was never allowed to sleep there. He'd wanted to remind her of what she couldn't have, what only he had the right to enjoy.

The rest of the ride was quiet. She was surprised when Asher's hand never strayed to touch her. The cloak wasn't much of a barrier, but he didn't attempt to breech it, not even when the fabric fell open. Did he not want her? She'd only had the old distorted mirror in the dungeon, so it was possible that eight months of not eating well and being kept out of the light had made her intolerable to look at. But why would he have bought her if that was the case?

Perhaps he had other plans. Maybe she wasn't to be used for sex at all. Maybe he needed a maid.

"We're here."

She looked out the window to see a house as grand as Lucas's had been, and she wondered what dark, dank dungeon she'd be introduced to next.

Grace followed him through the house as he gave her the tour. She knew he watched for her reaction, but how excited could she get about nice things she couldn't really touch or enjoy? She supposed she should embrace this brief bit of warmth and light for the few minutes it lasted. Asher told her about the history of the house as they went, but she remained silent, following along behind him, holding the cloak firmly around her.

Aside from the driver, she noticed one other servant in the place, a tall, lanky, middle-aged man with blond hair and kind eyes that had lines in the corners. When they reached the kitchen, he introduced himself.

"I'm William. If you need anything, just ask."

She looked quickly to Asher, but he just nodded. She had no idea what to do with that. If she needed anything? Was he serious? Was he planning on bringing her room service in the dungeon?

"Does she speak, sir?" William asked, confusion creasing his brow.

"Indeed she does. Just hasn't worked up to it yet. Give her time. It's new. She's scared."

Eight months ago, she would have been annoyed by even the idea of someone speaking in front of her as if she wasn't in the room. But that was then.

"Will you need me to prepare breakfast?" William asked.

"Not today," Asher said. "And I may let Grace take over some of the cooking."

"Very good, sir." William made a little bow and left them alone in the kitchen.

Grace stared at him. He knew her name. He'd *used* her name. That word that had become so disconnected, finally reattaching itself to her. For one brief moment she felt like a person. She might have enjoyed the feeling for longer, but Asher was leading her through the house again.

As they walked down a long hall, she berated herself. He'd just said her name. It wasn't as if he'd called her that directly. It didn't mean anything except that she'd become so piteous that hearing her name cross another person's lips was suddenly cause for celebration.

He took her through a study with dark wood paneling and walls of books. He pulled one out. She looked away when she saw the title of a kinky erotic novel. She wanted to forget she had a kink that could ever lead her into a situation like this. The bookcase shifted a little to reveal a door and steps going down.

Oh. The dungeon. *Now it begins.*

He was looking back at her now and seemed disappointed by something yet again. She could already see him returning her to Lucas and demanding his money back. She shuddered, thinking of what would become of her if that happened. Whatever the risk with Asher, she couldn't displease him enough to get sent back. At this point, either of them might kill her.

He held his hand out and she took it. Her feet were cold as he led her down the stone steps to the dungeon. It was nicer than the one Lucas had. There were several chests around the room as well as high-end bondage equipment. But even if it was nicer, it still had a cold, stone floor. And it still didn't have a window.

How long could she live without sunlight? Weren't all living things supposed to have sunshine? She'd grown pale the past few months, and she suspected she had a vitamin deficiency, partly due to how little she was fed, and partly due to being locked away all day in a window-less cell.

He let go of her hand and stepped back to let her explore the room. Her eyes fell on a bullwhip hanging on the wall. She took a few steps back when she saw it, just out in the open like it was his favorite. Asher's body stopped her retreat as she backed into him. His arms went around her, making her feel claustrophobic.

Instinctively she started to struggle, but almost the moment she did, his words rang out in her head: *Do. Not. Fight me.* And she went lax in his arms.

"Easy, kitten. I'm not going to use that on you."

Yeah, right. Then why was it down here? She wouldn't ask the question, of course. It had been ages since she'd communicated in any open way. Free verbal expression had been taken from her, leaving her only with her thoughts, running around and around in her head like a hamster on a wheel.

A part of her wished he'd give her some kind of speech rules, so she'd know what she could say and when. Some kind of *any* rules. This strange gentleness was too unnerving and uncertain. She kept waiting for the other shoe to drop, for him to grow bored with the ruse of being kind. For the real Asher to come out, the one she'd seen evidence of in Lucas's dungeon with those angry eyes.

He released her and his footsteps receded, starting up the steps. "Come," he said. "You don't want to stay here all day. It's too cold, especially with no shoes."

"What?" Somehow in her head she was going to manage to keep her mouth shut and not say a single word until she knew exactly what he expected from her, but the shock was too much. She'd assumed once they descended the stairs into the dungeon that the tour was over and he'd leave her there.

"So. She speaks." If not for the humor in his voice, she likely would have begged and cried and made a complete fool of herself.

Of course she wasn't staying in the dungeon right now. He'd said something about her cooking. He wanted a maid and a cook. He hadn't bought her for sex. He'd bought a domestic slave. He probably hadn't had to pay much, as eager as Lucas had seemed to sell her. Or maybe Lucas couldn't get much for her. A part of her was relieved he seemed to only want her for domestic duties, but another part was aware of just how far removed this was from the life she'd thought she was coming to, back when she'd been much more naïve.

"I'll show you your room now."

"Room?"

"Two whole words now," he teased her. "I think we're making progress already."

Grace followed him up the stairs, questions spinning through her head over whether he could possibly mean that she'd have a real room. It turned out to be on the second floor, across from his. In the grand scheme, it seemed less like a room and more like a studio apartment. It certainly wasn't like her room had been in her apartment before Eleu.

It wasn't set up as a bedroom, more of a sitting room. There was furniture, though no bed, and a closet, and a little bathroom. The carpet was soft and lovely. The room was warm and tastefully decorated with a vanity table, mirror, and bottles of perfumes and little containers of makeup along one wall. Another wall boasted a television. Sunlight filtered through windows and glass French doors that opened out onto a balcony with a lounger and table.

Please, God, let this not be a trick. Lucas had never gone this far to make her believe. She couldn't imagine the cruelty of a person who would go to this much trouble only to rip it all away. But Lucas had spent a whole year whispering naughty things to her over webcam, telling her all sorts of stories about what her life would be like, maintaining it so long that she'd believed what had seemed like honest eyes on the few occasions he'd shown her his face on the screen.

In hindsight, he'd given her so little opportunity to truly read him. He'd controlled their interactions from afar to a degree where she'd seen only what he'd carefully orchestrated for her to see. Was Asher doing the same thing? Would he build her hopes and her trust in him just so he could rip them down and watch and laugh as she cried? It seemed a high probability. Still, she couldn't help the feeling of gratitude that rushed into her, even for what was probably a short illusion.

If this could be true, she didn't even mind not having a bed. "If this is real . . . thank you." She couldn't help the tear that slipped down her cheek.

He cocked his head to the side and regarded her as if trying to determine what was going on in her head. The part of her that hoped this wasn't a lie, wished he could read her thoughts, because she couldn't imagine a situation in which she could ever trust him enough to truly express herself. No matter what he did, there was always another shoe that could fall.

"Get cleaned up and dressed. You can wear whatever you're comfortable in. There are clothes in the closets and PJs in the drawer. We aren't leaving the house today so whatever you want to wear right now is fine. Hurry, though. I want you to help me in the kitchen. Twenty minutes, all right?" He pointed, indicating the clock.

Grace stood there for a full minute as the second hand crawled over the numbers on the wall. It was too much for her brain to process. Clothes. Really? She tried not to get her hopes up too high. It could all be, and probably was, spank material slave-wear. It was unlikely she'd ever wear anything normal again. Still, being allowed some choice in something was . . . novel. There had been a time when she'd believed she'd wanted all choices removed from her.

But that hadn't been true. When confronted with a truly powerless reality, the *idea* had been hot and exciting, and perhaps if it had been a good man, someone who hadn't been intent on making her his torture toy in the literal sense, it would have been different. But the reality she'd been given instead drove home how valuable some freedoms were. Even the little ones.

"Grace?"

Her eyes flew to his, torn between the extreme gratitude of being addressed by name, as if she were a person, and fear that she'd be punished for standing there, gaping like a fish. *Think when you're alone, idiot. Not when he's standing right here.* Before she had time to work herself into a real panic, he spoke again.

"Do you understand what I just told you?" His voice was kind still, no anger apparent.

"Yes, Master," she squeaked out. She looked at the ground, unable to stand seeing what a devastating disappointment she must be. She didn't look up again until he'd left the room, shutting the door softly behind him.

When she was alone, she went to the walk-in closet and gaped at the contents. *What?* Either he was fucking with her head or she was dreaming. This couldn't be real. She wasn't sure which thought was more disturbing, that he was going to so much trouble to make her feel safe only to take it all away again, or that she might still be lying on the cold stone floor in Lucas's dungeon, dreaming all this.

The clothes were all normal. Stuff she might even have bought herself before the island. Grace closed her eyes against the vague memories of a time when she'd shopped. She hadn't thought before she'd stepped on that plane about never going shopping again. The simple idea of never picking out or buying her own clothes hadn't entered the fog of kink in her consciousness. She'd been too wrapped up in the fantasy and unconcerned with the practicalities, which she'd assumed would *work themselves out.*

Opening the drawers, she found actual pajamas. Pajama pants and cami tops. Not slut wear. Not slave wear. Of course, why would he dress her like a whore if that wasn't why he'd bought her? Still, William seemed to have a uniform. Why didn't she have a uniform? And why was he giving her the option of cooking and cleaning in pajamas to begin with? She couldn't wrap her head around any of it.

And how did he know her sizes? She had a vague memory of Lucas measuring her soon after she'd arrived, and noting the information down on some papers. Had that information been passed to Asher when he bought her? It must have. Otherwise she couldn't comprehend how he'd know her bra size and what size jeans to get. Though everything might be a little big. She'd lost some weight since arriving.

She picked pajamas. Though she was scared it was a trick, she couldn't resist the comfort of simple PJs. The bathroom was as lush and wonderful as the other room. She dropped the cloak once she was inside behind the locked door.

She'd hesitated about locking it. The idea of having the power to lock someone out, instead of being the one locked in was a new and exciting concept. She was afraid that if Asher came upstairs and found the door locked, she'd be in trouble she didn't want to think about. Her eyes drifted to the door in question.

The anxiety came over her in a wave, making her feel clammy, hot, cold. Her skin felt tight stretched across her, and she had to unlock the door. Just because she *had* a lock, didn't mean she was allowed to use it. And God help her if she did and he found out about it. Once the door was unlocked again, the anxiety receded until she was back to the normal, general level of fear she experienced all the time.

Grace didn't recall what it felt like not to be constantly afraid. But there was fear and there was panic. The former, when it was dull and constant, could be coped with. It could become the new normal, so you couldn't really remember what you'd felt like before. But the latter—there wasn't an acceptance for that level of fear.

She peeled the medical gauze and tape off her back and looked in the mirror. Everything had closed up at least, and it hurt a little less today. But those scars in between . . . She wiped the tears away when they started falling. If he only wanted a domestic servant, it wouldn't matter, and she'd be safe. But if he decided he wanted something else, when he saw those permanent marks on her, it would be over.

When she got to the kitchen, she found him standing behind the center island. While she was getting ready, he'd changed clothes, too. Now he was wearing a pair of pajama pants of his own. His upper body was bare and a study in sculpted perfection.

There was a time when the only thing she would have been able to think about was someone like this fucking or spanking her or ordering her around. She would have had an almost uncontrollable erotic compulsion to kneel at his feet, breathless with the desire to obey him. She wasn't sure what to feel right now.

He didn't seem to be an early riser. He must have gotten up earlier in order to come get her, even bypassing breakfast for the occasion.

Asher had taken out several bowls and spoons and pans. He smiled at her and she looked away, still unsure what he wanted. How was she supposed to act? Lucas had treated her like a prisoner from moment one. Her new master seemed to be treating her like a houseguest. At least for now. It was so confusing that she felt completely out of her element and unprepared for life in this new house.

"Grab a knife and dice up the tomatoes for the omelets," he said, pointing a spoon. He seemed to be mixing up a batch of muffins.

Her mouth watered at the sight of the fresh food, and she tried not to want it too much. He'd left a couple of smallish tomatoes and a knife beside a cutting board on the other end of the island from where he was mixing. Why was he letting her near a knife?

Briefly, a fantasy unfolded of slitting his throat and running. But it died there. The question that couldn't be stopped was—*And what then?* It wasn't as if he were the only thing that stood between her and freedom. What the fuck would she even do with freedom now?

Hesitantly, she moved toward the food. She stopped for a moment, unsure if they'd been washed off and if she was supposed to do that or just start chopping.

Batter was poured into muffin tins while she stood in indecision, afraid he'd yell at her if she did the wrong thing. He slid the pan into the oven and looked up. "You *do* understand the dicing concept, yes?"

"Yes, Master." She made a choice and started cutting the tomatoes into cubes. When he didn't complain, she relaxed a little. She actually missed cooking. After a moment, she was so involved in the activity that she didn't notice when he stepped behind her. His hand brushed against her ass, and she jumped, causing the knife to slip.

Grace backed away, holding her finger, a hiss of pain escaping her mouth, trying not to scream. This was bad. Very bad. He'd tried to touch her, and she'd pulled away from him. So stupid. Her finger was starting to throb but she was hyper-alert, her body protectively huddled for fear of whatever was coming next.

She was sure if she wasn't dreaming, the game was over and he'd fast-forward his plan to whatever the end goal was. She jumped again when he gently took her by the arm and led her to the sink.

"Hold it under the water until I get back."

Minutes passed and he returned with an antiseptic spray and bandages. He shut off the water, towel-dried her finger, calmly sprayed the cut, and bandaged it. She watched him, staying quiet. He wasn't yelling yet or punishing her, but that had to be next. Or soon. Maybe after he had his breakfast. She still didn't understand why he'd dismissed William from breakfast prep if he wasn't going to have her do it all.

He inspected the bandaging job, tossed the packaging away, and said, "You'll live. Go sit at the table while I finish cooking."

Then he went back to preparing the food as if nothing had happened. He took cheese and little ham cubes from the refrigerator to mix in the bowl with the eggs.

She was shaking now, waiting for that shoe to drop. The pleasant behavior wouldn't fool her. She'd seen it before. She'd never gotten away with a mistake before. He was waiting until after breakfast. Which meant there were all these minutes where the anticipation was just going to build higher, where she'd be in the panic place instead of the normal-level fear.

He started humming when he poured the eggs into the heated pans on the stove, and she couldn't take it anymore.

"Please, this slave is sorry."

He stopped and looked up. "Sorry for what?"

"Pulling away. This slave was only startled. It wasn't on purpose. Will you punish her?"

He made a face, and she wished she'd kept her mouth shut and waited it out. But she couldn't stand not knowing what was coming.

"You're not in trouble, kitten. But we do have to do something about your speech."

Was she not allowed to speak ever? Or only when spoken to? She had spoken first. So maybe that was the bad thing. Would she be punished for that instead? She couldn't ask now because if the answer was yes, that just added more punishment. Plus, maybe she was in trouble for not helping with breakfast now that she'd cut herself.

He continued, seemingly oblivious to her inner struggle. "But you understand you are mine, and I can touch you any time I want. Are we clear?"

"Yes, Master."

"Good girl."

She stopped breathing for a second. Those words she hadn't heard in so long. He couldn't know what they meant to her. How important they were to hear. Or maybe he did and it was all part of the plan . . . like what Lucas had done.

"Is your hand all right to set the table?"

"Yes, Master."

He pointed to the cabinets and the drawer with silverware. "Two plates, two glasses, and two forks and butter knives. Orange juice is in the fridge. You can go ahead and pour it."

She moved instantly to follow the orders, wondering who the other plate was for. Perhaps he had a lover? But were there free women on this island? Maybe he had a brother. Or maybe William ate breakfast with him. They seemed to have a conversational rapport. Hell, who knew how any other household on this island ran? She'd barely seen how Lucas ran his.

A part of her thought, obviously, that he was feeding her, too. She erased that thought immediately because she didn't want to start expecting good things here. It would just make it worse later.

When he put everything on the plates, she was still standing there, not sure what to do. Starving, but not wanting to do something both stupid and embarrassing. Embarrassing she'd survive, but stupid would just get her hurt. She was his slave. Of course she wasn't going to sit and eat at a table with him like a regular person. She couldn't even remember how to *be* a regular person.

He stared at her for a moment, then looked back to his plate. "Sit and eat. Eggs aren't good cold."

FIVE

A sher watched her from across the table as she ate. She was like a little mouse, so afraid and uncertain, as if he would take the food away at any second and scream at her for eating like he'd told her to. She'd been in his care only a couple of hours and already he wanted to kill Lucas.

He'd known the situation was bad from the coarse way her previous master allowed the other men at the showing to talk about his slave without the merest hint of anger, as well as the way he'd handled her and the state she'd been in. Especially those bandages peeking out from under her hair. That had been a dead giveaway.

And yet, having her here in his home, even for such a short period, he was suddenly overwhelmed with the reality and impossible state of the situation. She may never recover. Could he handle owning someone so damaged for the rest of her life or his?

Now that he truly understood how serious the damage was, and he suspected he still didn't grasp the half of it, he was even more convinced of his responsibility to her. But could either of them be happy that way?

He felt bad for the way he'd had to treat her down in Lucas's dungeon, but to show even a moment's weakness would have been disastrous.

Either party had forty-eight hours after the sale to change his mind. If Asher had given the impression he intended to be kind to her, the bastard would have stopped the sale. Lucas's end game was Grace dead or so broken she couldn't form a thought she hadn't been given express permission to think.

Whipping her right before the showing had been done deliberately to attract the type of brutal master he wanted to give her to, someone who would see her small remaining rebellion as an interesting challenge. Lucas could have just killed her, sure. But he liked money too much. If she could end up completely destroyed while his bank account got fatter it was win-win.

It was impossible to imagine how she would survive out in the world and equally impossible to imagine how a slave this broken had a future with any of the other men on the island. Eleu was a hedonist's paradise, and your average hedonist wasn't known for his self-sacrifice.

One thing was certain. Asher was going to have to get her on friendly speaking terms with personal pronouns. It made him cringe to hear her speak of herself in the third person as if she were some *thing*. The entire point of owning a slave, as opposed to a piece of furniture, was that they were a human being with thoughts and feelings and wants and needs. At least to his way of thinking.

He finally put his fork down, having made it through the omelet. The muffin still sat on his plate. "Grace." Her startled eyes rose to his. She did that every time he said her name, like she just couldn't believe the word still existed in the English language.

He sighed. "I'm going to ask you a question, and I need you to be completely honest with me. I can tell when people are lying." That was bullshit. He didn't always know when someone was lying, but it was imperative that she believe it so he could get enough information to know how to proceed with her. He had a feeling some of her fear and uncertainty were partly his fault, however inadvertent that might have been.

She just watched, waiting for the question.

"I haven't explained much to you yet or given you a lot of rules, and it occurs to me that this free-form way of dealing with you may be causing you added distress because you don't know what to expect from me. Would it be easier if I laid things out and gave you some ground rules to work with for now?"

Grace looked down at her plate, a tear trickling from the corner of her eye. She wiped it away quickly. If he could just get inside her head, it would be so much easier. He could guess some of it. Perhaps she was asking herself if this was a trick, if she was giving him ammunition to harm her. And he knew after the hell she'd just walked out of that no amount of soothing words would put her mind at ease. It would just take time. Watching her like this broke his heart, and he'd just brought her home. How many days, weeks, months could he go on living with someone with this level of fear toward him? Some fear turned him on, but they were quickly moving past the erotic zone.

No one said atonement, however weak the gesture, would be easy.

"Kitten, answer me. Would you like some structure and rules?"

Her hand was shaking as she put her fork down. "Please, don't make this slave answer . . ."

He got up and paced, unable to sit still. She flinched, and he hated that, but he needed to think and try to work out what was going on in her head. If he yelled and demanded, sure, she might comply, but she'd be more afraid. Maybe that was okay in the short term. Maybe she needed that firmness. Or maybe she'd lose the last little thread of her mind that was hanging on.

He turned toward her, then. "All right. Clearly this isn't working."

An almost manic look came over her. "Please don't take this slave back, she's very sorry. She . . ."

He stopped pacing and stared at her. No matter what he did or said she was obviously going to anticipate the worst possible result. Asher crossed the floor and pulled her out of the chair. He gripped her arms, careful not to hurt her, but unable to stop himself from making sure she absolutely understood his meaning.

"I will NEVER give you back to that monster. Do you understand me?"

"Yes, Master. This slave . . ."

"Stop."

She shut her mouth, her eyes filled with a terror he was sorry he had to put there.

"No more third person talk. You are a person, not a car or a desk or a piece of paper. Yes, you're my property, but you have an identity in there somewhere. I never want to hear you use the phrase: *This slave* or the word *she* when referring to yourself. You will use the words *I, me, my.* Are we clear?"

"Yes, Master." She was looking away from him now, looking so fragile and breakable that he couldn't stop himself from pulling her trembling body against him and wrapping his arms around her.

She held herself rigid for what felt like eons. Finally, something inside her seemed to uncurl and her body relaxed against him.

"Are you finished with your breakfast?"

She nodded, and he suspected she didn't trust her voice to speak. That was okay. The main concern on his mind was taking a look at what was under those bandages to see exactly how bad Lucas's last whipping had been. Asher took her hand and led her back up to her room.

The closer they got, the more tension seemed to crawl back inside her. He took a deep breath and looked her over when they arrived in the brightly lit room. It was a testament to how bad off she was that he was only now noticing how her erect nipples pushed against the fabric of the strappy, cotton top she'd chosen to wear.

The only reason she wouldn't wear a bra would be if the straps against her back hurt too much. Perhaps another type of slave, who hadn't been so utterly broken, would have gone bra-less with a different intention. But Grace didn't seem to have the presence of mind or even the desire to seduce.

Looking at her now, he knew he wouldn't be able to resist her. And why should he? He'd paid good money for her. She had no rights except those he chose to give her. If circumstances had been different and he'd been the one to meet her online instead of Lucas, she'd be horny and willing. He knew he wasn't an unattractive man. But Grace was too scared to want him, and he didn't know how to move her out of that frightened place and into one where he wouldn't feel like a monster for taking what was his to take.

He hadn't thought he'd have a mental war between law and ethics on his hands. It had seemed like a simple enough transaction at the time. He didn't regret the choice, yet it wasn't as simple as the fantasy of rescue.

Asher stood back, assessing, trying to figure out how to do this without freaking her out more. Her arms were crossed defensively over her chest, and she was looking at the floor. So quiet. What had she been like before coming to Eleu? How much of her identity had Lucas destroyed forever, and how much could Asher bring back?

"How long did you talk to Lucas online before he convinced you to come here?" he asked. As he'd watched her, he'd become aware of the fact that while he knew how long Lucas had her, he wasn't aware of the time frame leading up to it.

"A year and six days." Her voice came out so soft, like a whisper carried by wind. At first he wasn't sure he'd heard her. It was only after the phrase was fully uttered that his mind was able to process it and feed it back to him as something coherent.

"Fuck," he said under his breath.

Of course she jumped again. Everything he did made her jump. He wondered if he shouldn't just give her a few days in the house free from his presence, let William bring her meals and see how that went. But somehow he knew such an action would only heighten her uncertainty. The sooner he could get her into a routine, the better.

"Turn around."

Her eyes flew to his, questioning if she'd done or said something wrong.

"It's okay."

She still hesitated for a moment, but it was a quick moment. He couldn't calculate how fast she must have flipped through the emotions of fear over what he would do to her when she complied and fear of what he would do to her if she didn't. And there was no way to soften this or make it easier.

Her golden hair fell in thick curls that ended right above the curve of her hips. He moved behind her and swept it over her shoulder.

"Did he tell you pretty lies online for that year about how your life would be?"

"Yes, Master."

He could hear the tears in her voice as she forced the words out of her mouth. Of course she must think he was toying with her, but he had to know how bad this was.

"He made you believe you'd have lovely things and live kinkily ever after, didn't he?"

She hesitated a moment and then said, "Yes, Master."

Why the hesitation there? At that particular question? "But . . . ?" he said, leading her, hoping she'd reveal the impulse that had made her pause in her answer.

"He said he wouldn't be an easy master."

There it was.

"So you believe all this is your fault? Everything he's done to you? Because he warned you, and you still got on the plane?"

She nodded.

He wanted to tell her it wasn't her fault but it seemed wasted verbiage at this point. She wasn't going to believe anything he said right now.

He sighed. Before he could talk himself out of it, he did what he'd made her turn around for. He took the edges of the top and lifted and pulled it over her head, tossing the fabric to the floor.

Asher cursed under his breath. Her back was a mess. So many scars that would never go away to erase the memory of Lucas from her. And the new marks. They'd closed but they were still very red, probably quite tender. He winced, thinking of how he'd held her in the kitchen and how part of the reason she'd tensed might have been pain, not just fear.

He was so morbidly transfixed by the awful sight in front of him that he didn't notice the change in her breathing, the signals that her anxiety had peaked and they were moments away from a scene of epic proportions.

"Please, Master, this slave is sorry . . ."

There had been more she seemed prepared to say in her bid for mercy, but he cut her off. "Grace—what did we say about third person?"

"I . . . I'm sorry," she corrected.

"Sorry for what?" He had his suspicions over what her litany of apologies was about, but he needed to hear it from her. The more he could get her to tell him directly, the less he had to play mind reader.

"The . . . the scars. You paid money for . . . this sl . . . for me, and I'm marked." It was a real struggle for her to shed the speech patterns Lucas had no doubt beaten into her. Asher wondered which scars had taught her the lesson he most wanted to undo.

"Then isn't that my fault? If I wanted you perfect and unmarked, should I not have inspected my potential property before acquiring it?"

She was quiet for a long moment.

"Answer."

"No, Master."

"I shouldn't have?"

"Yes! This sl . . . I don't know what you want from me. Please don't hurt her . . . me." Clearly unable to take the close proximity of the threat, she moved away from him until she was cowering in a corner.

Oh no. He wasn't having that. "Come here."

The tick of the wall clock seemed to be the only sound left in the world as she slowly moved back to him. With her top on the floor and no bra underneath, she was bare to his gaze, her hair having slipped behind her during her retreat. If she weren't so broken, there were a million other things he could think to do with her right now, but he resisted, knowing how important it was to lay this groundwork now.

When she reached him, he stroked the side of her face, trying to calm her and hoping Lucas hadn't used a similar gesture when playing fake trust-building games with her. "I expect honesty from you. Never a lie. I will never harm you for telling me the truth, no matter how awful you think it is. Do you understand, kitten?"

"Yes, Master."

"Good girl." He helped her back into the top and could see the confusion on her face because he wasn't touching her. He was pretty confused about it, too. And maybe he should touch her. He certainly was within his rights to. And he'd have to very soon, but not right now.

"I'm going to ease you slowly in, but I am going to train you. And I will be firm. What I won't be is abusive. Lucas sold you because he couldn't really own you. He could break you, yes. But you never gave every piece of yourself to him. There are parts of you he could never touch. He said as much when I came for you and was standing out in the hallway. But you will give *me* everything. You won't give it because you're afraid of me. You'll give it because you're grateful and because you trust me. I don't care how long it takes us to get to that point. But we will get there."

Grace was still processing everything he'd said. Part of her wanted to trust every word, but every time one part of her mind tried to let her, another part chastised her for being so stupid and falling into what must be a trap. What would happen to her when she couldn't give him everything like he'd just said she would?

She'd gone back to looking at the floor because it felt safer than trying to figure out what was going on behind those stormy blue eyes of his. She knew he was watching her, assessing, cataloging, trying to figure something out. She could feel his stare on her.

"Is there someone you'd like to call?"

Her eyes snapped up. "Call?"

He took a cell phone out of his pocket. "Surely you have family or friends back home you'd like to speak to. Someone you miss?"

Why was he doing this? Why was he dangling these carrots? "Please don't do this . . ." She just wanted him to be however he was going to be. No games. No pretending. If she let herself believe in this and then he took it away . . .

He arched a brow. "Don't do what? Don't let you call someone? Don't be decent? Tell me what you want, in plain speech. I don't need a title this second. Just tell me exactly what it is that you most want right now."

She took a breath. "Just be real. This sl . . . I . . . I can't do this again. I can't believe in something that isn't a nightmare only to have it torn away again. Please, please, just be real. Keep me in the dungeon or beat me or whatever it is you want, but don't pretend to be kind."

The look he gave her was so far outside her recent experience that she didn't know how to categorize it, at least not on any face but her own on the few occasions she'd made the mistake of looking at her reflection in Lucas's dungeon. She shut her eyes tight, to block out the look he gave her.

Grace startled when hands closed around her arms.

"Look at me," he commanded.

She opened her eyes. His expression was fierce, but it didn't seem angry. Not like what she'd seen that morning when he'd stepped into the dungeon. The thought came over her suddenly that maybe he hadn't been angry at her at all. Maybe it was something else.

"I am real. This room is real. The breakfast you just ate is real. None of this is a game or a trick. I know you don't believe that yet, but you will believe it in time. Now do you have someone you want to call?"

"No, Master."

He let go of her and sat on the sofa. "You have no family or friends?"

"My brother is a drug addict. I worked a lot of hours, so I just had one good friend, Lainey."

"So call her."

"She tried to convince me not to come here. I couldn't . . . I can't . . ."

He nodded. "You don't have to explain. I think I understand. How about the Internet? Could you email or instant message her?"

She thought about it. "I think so."

Asher stood and extended a hand. She tentatively put her hand in his and allowed herself to be led across the hall. His room was opposite from hers in every way. Whereas hers was bright and colorful and inviting, his was dark and intimidating.

The walls were done in rich, dark wood paneling. Heavy drapes blocked the light from the windows. He crossed the floor and pulled the thick fabric back to let the sunlight in. A king-sized bed stood against one wall. The headboard consisted of metal bars, perfect for chaining someone down.

In another life, standing in a room with such an attractive, dominant force of a man, she would have fantasized about him chaining her to the bed and having his wicked way with her. Now the thought scared her. She'd experienced too much real pain and fear to see it as a sexual game anymore. And yet her body still perversely responded.

There was a small desk on one side of the room and a laptop. He sat in the leather, swivel chair and booted up the computer. Then he pulled up a folder. "If your messenger service isn't one of these, you can go online and download it. I'll give you some privacy to chat or email. Come join me when you're finished."

Giving her privacy didn't mean leaving the room, only that he wasn't going to hover over her while she typed. Instead, he propped some pillows against the headboard and turned on a flat-screen television to a sports channel.

He seemed so normal. What if she just tried to believe in him? For a little while. The worst that could happen is he'd take everything away. Maybe she should embrace whatever small kindnesses he offered, then if they ended, she wouldn't have to berate herself for wasting it all waiting for that other shoe.

Finally, she settled in the chair and searched through the folder to find the link to her messenger service. Lainey worked in a small advertising office that didn't monitor Internet activity as much as some of the larger firms. She usually kept her messenger on all day.

Grace entered her screen name and password, shocked she could still remember it. She hadn't been on a full minute when Lainey messaged her.

StrawberryLaine: Grace? Is that you? Are you okay?

She took a deep breath. This was exactly why she couldn't do this on the phone. The second those words came out of Lainey's mouth, Grace would have broken down in sobbing fits.

Gracie343: It's me. I'm fine.

StrawberryLaine: I haven't heard anything from you for almost a year! I went to the police, and when I told them about the island they thought I was insane. Making it up. They'd never heard of it, of course. And I didn't know exactly where it was so I couldn't point them in the right direction. I didn't know if your plane crashed or you were murdered or . . .

Gracie343: I'm okay.

She stared at the screen for a long time. She'd have to tell her the truth, or some version of it. After all that worrying and mourning, Lainey deserved some answers. Grace waited for more questions or accusations. Maybe she'd been called away for a moment. She was at work after all. Another few minutes passed before Lainey finally replied.

StrawberryLaine: Well, what happened? This better be good. I was so worried. If you just decided to lose track of time and . . .

Gracie343: Lucas was a bad guy. You were right.

StrawberryLaine: Oh. Oh my God. Are you still with him? How did you get to a computer?

Gracie343: He sold me. Asher, my new master, let me use the computer.

StrawberryLaine: Has he hurt you? The new one?

Gracie343: Not yet.

StrawberryLaine: How long have you been with him?

Gracie343: A few hours.

StrawberryLaine: Do you want to come home?

Gracie343: He won't let me go.

StrawberryLaine: We could find a way . . . The police didn't believe me before, but I can give them the chat logs.

Gracie343: No.

StrawberryLaine: What do you mean, no?

Gracie343: I'm different, Lainey. I can't . . . There's no . . . If Asher is real, maybe this is the best place for me.

StrawberryLaine: What do you mean if he's real?

Gracie343: Just leave it alone, okay?

StrawberryLaine: I'm sure there's a way we can track your location just from being on the Internet.

Gracie343: I need to go. I'll talk to you later if he lets me.

StrawberryLaine: Grace, wait.

StrawberryLaine is typing . . .

She logged out before Lainey could say more. Grace clicked the laptop lid shut and moved over to the bed. She had no idea what he wanted. Stand? Kneel? Get in the bed?

"That didn't take very long."

She just stood, staring down at her hands. An awkward silence descended between them, and then he spoke again.

"I know you've been abused in every way imaginable and that right now you don't know if more is coming, but when I do something nice for you, I expect manners. I expect you to say thank you."

"Thank you, Master." She looked up when she heard his hand patting the bed. He'd pulled back the covers beside him.

"Undress and get in."

She couldn't stop the tears that started to move down her cheeks.

"Grace."

She looked up.

"I'm not going to harm you, but the sooner we at least partly cross this bridge, the easier things will go. I've been thinking while you were on the computer. I don't know if my way of dealing with this is the best way, considering your history. But it's the way I've decided to proceed. I know perhaps it's selfish. But I bought you for many reasons. I want a sexual companion. If I were just some guy on the street who wanted to date you, then perhaps this would be evil and insensitive. But I'm not just some guy. I'm your master."

So maybe he hadn't bought her just to clean his house or cook his meals. Grace didn't know how she felt about that, but she did know she was getting stupid. He was patiently waiting. Not yelling or screaming or grabbing her and throwing her down. He was waiting for her to make the choice to come to him. But that only made it harder and made her feel more responsible somehow for whatever happened next. Irrational though that was.

With Lucas there had been none of that. There had been demands and either immediate obedience or swift and painful punishment. Sometimes punishment had included missed meals and sensory deprivation. A few hours away from that, and she was already hesitating because so far hesitating hadn't earned her pain.

"Don't force me to punish you on your first day."

Those words made her blood run cold. So like what Lucas had told her when she'd hesitated for a moment about giving him the ring. Asher was the same. Of course he was the same. Why would she believe he wasn't the same?

But he hadn't punished her *yet*. Maybe he wouldn't look for imaginary reasons to beat her. If she just gave him whatever he wanted, maybe she could delay punishments for a while. After all, there were differences between them, weren't there? Lucas had burned away all her memories in the first twenty minutes and locked her in a cell. Asher had given her nice clothes, a warm shower, a good breakfast, and contact with her only friend in the outside world. But Lucas had built her trust for a year online . . .

"Last chance, Grace."

His voice had gone down a register, sounding almost like it had in Lucas's dungeon. There was that scary edge that compelled her to obedience. It worked again now as she peeled the clothing off and climbed into bed.

Asher lay back against the pillows. "Straddle me, kitten. I don't want you on your back until it heals."

She could feel his erection straining against his pajamas into the space between her legs as she obeyed the order. One of his arms wrapped around her waist, just missing the marks Lucas had left, and the other gently grasped the back of her neck, pulling her to him. When his lips pressed against hers, his tongue demanding entrance into her mouth, she gasped.

Inexplicably, her body responded to him. She could feel the wetness building. After everything that had transpired with Lucas, no part of her should want this. Even though Asher hadn't hurt her, it was . . . perverse. She couldn't even tell him no. She didn't even have the *right* to tell him no. And if she did, surely he wouldn't listen. It would be bad. So why did she have to physically stop herself from rubbing against him?

She wasn't able to contain the tears that started until they became pained sobs. Asher stopped, pulling back from her, and she tensed, waiting for pain to be delivered. How dare she interrupt his sexual experience with her trauma.

"Grace, look at me."

Her eyes fluttered open.

"Tell me *exactly* why you're crying. And don't be cute about it. I know why, but I want to know exactly why. I need to know everything that triggers you. I need to be completely inside your head. And if you even think about lying to me, I will know."

She shuddered at that last part. Every time he wanted her to tell him something, he said he would know if she lied. And she believed him. It was too big of a risk not to believe him. And she didn't know what to do with this because Lucas had never made these kinds of demands. He'd just wanted to use her and wanted her to obey. He couldn't have cared less what she was thinking. She knew even now that Asher would own her fully because he was willing to make demands to get inside her thoughts, and she was too afraid not to give him everything he wanted to know. If he turned on her, it would be worse than it had been with Lucas.

She took a breath. "This sl . . ." She faltered under the sharp look he gave her. It was so hard to speak about herself in first person with him. He couldn't begin to imagine how hard. Lainey was the only person with whom it had been easy. But with a man who had complete power over her, it felt foreign and odd. And uncomfortable. "—I mean I . . . I'm wrong. I'm not just broken. I'm *wrong*. Things that shouldn't turn me on, turn me on. Even when Lucas punished her . . . me . . . sometimes, I got wet. And now . . . I don't know you. And I'm . . . responding. It's wrong."

He pulled her down against his chest, stroking her hair. "Lucas used your needs against you. But you aren't *wrong*. There is nothing wrong with you or how you're wired. The only thing wrong is how Lucas used it to hurt you. I'm glad your body wants me. It's okay to just give me your body and your obedience for now. The rest will come in time."

He slid a hand between her legs to feel her wetness. "This, I can work with."

She blushed when her hips pressed harder against his probing fingers.

Suddenly Asher wasn't just *theoretically attractive*. Though she struggled with an uncountable number of conflicting thoughts and feelings, she couldn't deny that she did find him appealing, and her body agreed. She was still sure everything would be ripped away and something bad would happen any minute. But for now, for just this one moment, she was so grateful to be feeling something pleasant, that she was willing to surrender to it and try not to think too hard about anything coming after.

Like the sex, what would happen when he was inside her? Was it going to feel like rape? Like Lucas? She squeezed her eyes shut, as if by doing so she could shut out the noise in her brain. At the same time, Asher started stroking the folds of her sex, dipping inside her and using her moisture to massage her already swollen clit.

Her breathing came heavier and faster as all those awful thoughts blanked out, and then a minute later, she came. He moved his hand out from between her legs and let her collapse on top of him.

Oh God, oh God, oh God. The yelling in her mind kept getting louder. Was she in trouble for that? He hadn't given her permission. Lucas almost never let her come, except in circumstances where he felt making her come would be more awful and shameful than not letting her. Surely this wasn't acceptable. She should have asked. But it had happened so fast, too fast to think.

"It's been a long time for you, hasn't it?" he said.

"Yes, Master."

She didn't beg this time. Already she was developing a new strategy where Asher was concerned. If he heard her beg every second of every day, he'd become so desensitized to it, that when she actually needed mercy, it wouldn't penetrate. Maybe it wouldn't anyway, but if she could hold back and not beg so much, she might have an ace to play later. At least she shouldn't beg until the moment before he seemed about to do something horrible. Right now they were just laying there, his erection wedged between her legs, hard and large, with only the material of his pajamas barring his entry. And even after the orgasm, she wanted to rub against him.

He was wrong: there was nothing okay about the way she responded to things. Without that weakness, she never would have come to Eleu to begin with. She'd be safe and happy, living a normal life with a normal job in the normal world. Not laying here, helpless to protect herself, hoping her new master could really be decent, that it wasn't some trick.

She was so exhausted. She was tired from getting such poor sleep and so little nutrition in the dungeon. She was tired from all the fear. She felt like she'd gone non-stop on adrenaline for so long until her ability to produce it had just stopped. She'd been running on fumes, just trying to survive for weeks—if not months. Suddenly everything in her body gave out, and if Asher said anything else, it didn't slip past the barrier of unconsciousness for her to hear it.

Six

Asher stood in the kitchen, having downed his third cup of coffee because it felt too early for alcohol. Perhaps he should amend that rule. After her orgasm, he'd felt the light trembling, as if she was afraid she'd done something wrong. But she was quiet, retreating back into her head.

Which was when he felt like an evil bastard.

The unfortunate reality was that there was no real way to know the best course to take with her. He couldn't simultaneously try two different methods, and he was still convinced his way was right in the long run. She was his, damn it. And he wasn't harming her.

He hadn't fucked her, and wouldn't have even if she hadn't fallen asleep on top of him. It was too soon. But it didn't mean he wouldn't touch what belonged to him. He'd waited until she'd drifted deeper into sleep and her breathing had evened before slipping from the bed. He'd covered her with the blanket and shut off the light on his way out the door.

His erection was still raging. She thought *she* was wrong? He was the one who got a hard-on every time she looked up at him with those desperate, brown eyes. Everything in his brain screamed: *Prey. Take. Use.* He wasn't exactly proud of it, but there it was. He hadn't even felt this way with Darcy. And he'd loved Darcy.

Lucas wasn't the only one who told pretty lies. Asher had been lying to himself since the moment he'd decided he was going to take Grace to atone. He'd been kidding himself thinking he wasn't ready to move on. He was ready. He hadn't just wanted a slave who he may or may not bed. He'd wanted a lover, and he'd perhaps selfishly taken one who was too damaged to want that as much as he did. At the same time, he couldn't deny the fact that selfish intentions or no, he *had* rescued her from a much worse fate.

"You fucker."

William stood in the doorway, his arms crossed over his chest. He'd dropped the polite and civilized butler routine. Asher sighed. Of course William would be lurking nearby. That was his way. The only reason it hadn't gotten him fired and deported was that he wasn't just a butler, he was a friend.

William didn't wait for a verbal acknowledgment. Clearly he felt his moral outrage trumped the propriety of his station in the house. "Why not just throw her down and rape her? You think molesting her is a solution to the trauma she's already suffered?"

"She didn't seem to be that upset about it while I was doing it."

"She had no choice!"

"She's a slave. Slaves don't get choices! Darcy was a slave," Asher said.

"But Darcy still had a personality. She wasn't terrified. It was her kink."

"And it's Grace's kink, too."

William shook his head. "No. This is wrong."

Asher rounded on him, growing weary of the insubordination. "Is it? If I'd treated Darcy more like property, she'd still be alive. But no, I was weak with her. She pushed too far. People talked. I had to get control of her, and instead of doing it myself, I gave the responsibility to someone else."

Sure, he'd just been berating himself, but now that his butler was doing it, he found it easier to come up with endless rationalizations to prove he was the good guy. "I'm not going to buy someone and keep them like a cloistered nun. You honestly expect me to keep a beautiful woman in my home—a woman I own, I might add— and never touch her?"

"I . . . sir . . . but you knew the state she was in. If you'd wanted that, you could have bought someone else."

"And then what would happen to Grace? I'm the best option she has, and you know it. You can be as self-righteous as you want to be. She's safe with me. If I treat her like she's broken, she may never recover, but if I treat her like any other slave, then maybe there's a chance."

William still had a disapproving look on his face, and Asher wanted to knock it right off. But he refrained.

"I still think you should give her time to—"

"She's got to come to me emotionally in her own time, but I will have her body and her obedience on my time. That's what makes me the master and her the slave."

William would have continued his argument if not for the crash out in the hallway.

"Grace—?" By the time Asher got through the door, she'd already flown up the stairs. "Fuck. This vase was my grandmother's. Clean that up, will you, William? It's too far gone to glue together, but save me one of the larger pieces."

William looked white as a sheet. "Sir . . ."

"Oh for God's sake. I'm not going to beat her. Just because I'm learning my lessons from Darcy doesn't mean I've had a personality transplant." He shook his head, disgusted, and left William to take care of the shattered vase.

At the top of the stairs, he stood in a moment of indecision looking between his door and Grace's. He started toward his bedroom, then stopped and rethought it. Why should he have to turn the house upside down looking for her?

He took a few steps back and raised his voice. "Grace, you've got exactly thirty seconds to come out."

In less than ten, she shot out of his room and was on her knees in front of him. Seeing her in that position, so quick to obey, reminded him sharply of the fact that his needs hadn't been taken care of. Asher took a slow breath, trying to steady himself. He could feel himself becoming drunk on the power. Darcy had never been this quick to obey.

Darcy hadn't been terrorized by a monster for months either, you twit.

He and Grace were some pair. Both of them completely and utterly *wrong*. He was surprised she didn't beg, though she was crying as quietly as she could.

"You shouldn't listen in on conversations that aren't your business, kitten."

"This slave is sorry, she woke up and heard yelling and was scared—"

"What did we say about third person?"

"I . . . I'm sorry. Please . . ."

"Tell me what you're afraid of right now."

There was a pause. He watched her, waiting for her to comply or try to bullshit him, but it was obvious from her tense posture that she'd tell him whatever he wanted to know.

"I'm scared you're going to beat me or take the room away from her . . . me and make me stay in the dungeon, or that I won't eat for a few days, or—"

"Stop."

She closed her mouth. He knelt beside her and pulled her into his arms. At first she resisted, but then she allowed herself to be held.

"I will never punish you by taking away food. In the first place, you're so malnourished, it's amazing you made it down the stairs and back up again unassisted. In the second place, it's just plain fucked up. The dungeon is too dark and cold. I'm not tossing you in there, either. Someday I will physically punish you, but not today. It would do more damage than good right now. But I *am* going to punish you."

He could feel her flinch and pull in on herself, wondering what awful thing he'd do that she hadn't immediately thought of. Asher stood and pulled her up with him, then took her back into her room and settled her on a couch. He rifled through a drawer and came out with a notebook with lined paper and a couple of pens.

She looked quizzically at him, the bizarreness of being handed a notebook overwhelming her fear.

"You are going to write the following sentences three hundred times." He arched a brow waiting for her to open the notebook. In another situation, he might have laughed at the expression on her face: a strange mixture of relief, gratitude, and shock. But it wasn't funny for many reasons.

When her pen was poised over the first line, he said: "I will never again eavesdrop on my master, nor will I run from him when he calls my name. I am very sorry I displeased him in this way, and I will try very hard not to do it again."

The punishment served two purposes. It was fairly unpleasant to do the same monotonous activity that many times, so it was a deterrent. Most importantly, it might help her with her pronoun issue. "I want you to number them, and I want it legible. It'll take several hours, so you may take a break for lunch. William will bring you something."

"Yes, Master. Thank you."

"I'm sure you won't still be thanking me when you're done." The one time he'd introduced a similar punishment to Darcy, she'd whined so much about it that he'd had to paddle her anyway. And it still hadn't stopped the behavior. As much as he'd loved her, he'd found it endlessly irritating how much she whined about any punishment that wasn't *sexy*. She'd never really internalized the idea of herself as his real property. Even with laws surrounding them that said so. And to be honest, he hadn't either.

Grace hadn't let out even the mildest protest at writing lines. He thought she might actually *still* thank him when it was over—and mean it. Even as much as her hand would hurt by then.

He watched her for a moment, sitting there in the pajamas she'd been wearing earlier in the morning, carefully copying over the sentences into the notebook. His cock twitched in his pants. He left before he did something stupid and rash.

His intentions to hold off from consummating things with her were weakening by the moment. Asher crossed the hall to the bathroom and shut and locked the door. He shucked his clothes and got underneath the spray. He'd had a shower before going to pick her up, of course. Right now he just wanted to wank, and the bathroom was the only place to do it in complete privacy.

He knew Grace would stay in her room and do as he'd ordered, but William was a whole different matter. The last thing he wanted was for his butler to walk in on a mid-morning wank in the bedroom.

Closing his eyes, he replayed the morning from the moment he'd walked into Lucas's dungeon. Those frightened eyes, the absolute desperation she had to please him. So unlike Darcy. He should be repulsed by making such comparisons. He should feel guilty for being so turned on by his entire exposure to Grace. She was so broken. That shouldn't get him off. Although he was angry with the way Lucas had treated the girl and the horrible conditions she'd been kept in, the resulting desperation to please and obey aroused him to a degree he hadn't been prepared for.

Wrong wrong wrong wrong wrong pounded in his head in a staccato beat, matching the rhythm of the shower spray and his hand jerking on his cock.

He bit back the groan as he came so it wouldn't carry across the hallway, then pressed his palms against the tiles, leaning forward. He let his breath settle back into the normal pattern as the evidence of his orgasm swirled down the drain. Why did it matter if Grace heard him? Did he not have the right to come in his own house? He should be using her for that purpose anyway. It's what he'd bought her for.

The same thing that he'd claimed had drawn the *lowest common denominator* to want to buy her, was what drove him as well. But with less sinister intentions. Grace was a slave who truly was a slave. She wasn't an online fantasy girlfriend who'd come over for kinks and thrills that he couldn't bring himself to punish in any meaningful way. She was someone he'd never *have* to punish that way. Someone who would give her absolute loyalty and obedience out of gratitude.

Perhaps it was the gratitude that stirred his blood the most. And that wasn't so wrong, was it?

He let the shower run for ten more minutes, not washing off, just standing there, letting the water slide down his skin. It was more subterfuge. If he was in and out too fast, both William and Grace would know what he'd been up to. And again, he didn't know why he cared so much. He'd masturbated the previous day. And the day before that. And the day before that. It wasn't necessarily all about the abused woman in the room across the hall, obediently writing out her punishment sentences.

Oh hell, it had been about her from the moment he'd seen her at the showing. She'd triggered both his cock and his protective urges in such a dramatic way he would have paid two million for her. More. And he was terrified that, rather than atone, he would somehow become a greater monster because of his lack of self-control with this one. He just wanted her too much.

Grace was on number one hundred twenty when the knock sounded on the door. Her hand had just started cramping, and she was relieved to put the pen down for a break. It felt too odd to say "come in," as if she had any rights to deny anyone entrance into a room that wasn't really hers. So she just stayed silent and waited. She hadn't heard much of the argument, but she'd heard enough to know William was against slavery, which made him seem safer. The door bumped open and the butler smiled kindly at her.

"I brought you some homemade potato and corn chowder and grilled cheese."

Her mouth watered at the sight of the tray. Fresh, warm food. Not cold scraps. It was still a hard thing to get used to. A wonderful thing to get used to, but hard. William's extreme reaction against Asher caused her to hold out hope that she had an ally in this house and that maybe she wouldn't have everything good stripped away, that it wasn't some game.

She couldn't believe that after only a few hours out of Lucas's dungeon, she was hoping for something better, allowing herself to believe in it for even a moment.

William set the tray on the elegant table in front of the couch. "If you need anything else, you can use the call box." He pointed to a little rectangle set into the wall beside the flat screen. She hadn't noticed the intercom, but then she hadn't spent much time in the room to explore every inch of it. She'd spent most of her time inside her head since she'd gotten here.

When she didn't say anything, the butler turned to leave.

"He didn't hurt her . . . I . . . I mean me. Earlier. He didn't hurt me."

He stopped in the doorway and gave her that look people give abused puppies and trauma victims, as if they're so damaged they can't possibly know their own minds. It made a little part of her way down deep inside—angry. Angry that someone thought she didn't know her mental state and couldn't express her own feelings correctly. But the thought quickly receded because defiant thoughts hadn't been safe for a long time. And Lucas had trained her well.

"It's none of my business, of course," the butler said.

But it was suddenly very important to Grace. "He didn't hurt me," she repeated. "If you knew the things she endured in that dungeon with her other master . . . you wouldn't . . . ." She'd lapsed back into the third person speech without realizing. Even though she'd written two hundred and forty sentences in which she'd written *I* and *my* so much they should have stuck. But she was running on emotion right now, not careful thought.

"I apologize if my words upset you," William said.

It took a moment for her to process that someone had actually issued an apology to her. She could have spent the whole day in awe over that one thing, but she had to get the rest out. "If he could . . . if he could be like this, like he is now, most of the time . . . this sl . . . I mean I . . . could maybe be okay." Then she asked the question she had to know the answer to because it was the one thing that made her fear Asher might be worse than Lucas. "Did my master kill his last slave? There were rumors he did."

The butler's eyes widened a little. "How did you hear about that?"

"Lucas. Is it true?" She had to work to keep her voice from shaking and the tears from falling again. "Did he kill her?"

William shook his head. "She died, but it was an accident. Not by his hand. He was a wreck for months. Barely left his room. Barely ate. He's just now gotten his weight back to normal."

The butler could be lying. She knew that. It wasn't as if she was a stranger to convincing lies. But something in his eyes, coupled with the argument she'd overheard, made her want to trust him. If it were true, she might be safe, and not as part of some ruse to make breaking her again more fun. Really, truly safe. For the first time in Eleu.

The sobs that wracked her body then were sobs of relief, gratitude, and hope. Asher may have just saved her, for what reason she didn't know, but she couldn't stop the emotion as it bubbled out. The butler was still standing in the doorway, watching her crack up. He had a confused look on his face, as if trying to flip through everything that had been said to see what set her off.

"I'm sorry. I didn't mean to upset you, Grace."

And more tears, because her name was becoming a normal utterance around here. She shook her head. "I'm not upset. It's too hard to explain." She looked helplessly up at him, hoping somehow she could just transfer what she was feeling into his brain without the complication of words that would only make her cry harder.

He nodded and quickly excused himself.

She stared at the food on the tray and the glass of iced water with a bowl of lemons on the side. So much trouble gone to for her so she could eat. She wondered if Asher had the same lunch and if he'd eaten it alone in the kitchen, or in his office, or in the bedroom with the big TV, watching sports.

She glanced at the television in her own room and clicked it on, flipping the channels until she got to the cartoon channel. Here she was, eating a real meal in comfortable pajamas, curled up on a soft sofa, watching cartoons while the sunlight streamed in her window. Could any of this be real? She found the anxiety and dread creeping in again that it was all a dream and that she'd wake up any minute back where she'd been a few hours ago. Because she couldn't possibly be this lucky.

Later, she was back to writing her sentences, the cartoons still humming on low in the background. She didn't notice when the door opened. Grace looked up to find Asher watching her.

Her anxiety returned. Had she gotten too comfortable? Was she doing something wrong?

"William is working in the garden, and I thought I'd grab the tray and check on you."

She remained silent, still unsure how to behave.

He glanced back at the television and then at her again, and she tensed. "Are you able to concentrate on what you're writing with the television on?"

"Yes, Master," she said. "Do you want . . . me to turn it off?" She'd had to think, to carefully form her words and make sure she was speaking correctly and not lapsing back into that awful third person speech.

"If you can concentrate, you can leave it on in the background." Then he was gone.

A few hours later he returned again. By this time her hand hurt so much she could barely move it across the page.

"What number are you on?"

"Two fifty-two." She'd promised herself she was going to stop all the stupid blubbering and crying about everything, but it really hurt, and she couldn't stop the stray tears that escaped and ran down her cheek. She quickly wiped them away with the back of her hand before they could wet the paper she was writing on.

"Stop," he said.

"But . . . I can finish." Was he upset she wasn't done yet? Was she in trouble? Her muscles tensed, poised. For what she didn't know. The next words to come out of his mouth caused the tension to flow back out of her again.

"I know you can, but I'm asking you to stop. You will finish, but not today. You're in too much pain. It's time to take care of you."

She wanted to finish the lines. She'd been so close to completing the task, that it felt like she'd somehow failed him to stop so close to the end. But she didn't protest, partly because she wasn't really sure if she physically *could* complete it right now, and partly because he'd just told her to stop, and she wasn't about to argue with a direct order. Since the conversation with

William all she wanted was to please her master. Not because she was trying to appease to delay punishment but because if this was real, the only thing important to her was obeying the man who had made it real.

"Thank you, Master." She put the pen down on the table, and he smiled. The smile warmed and lit her up inside.

He clicked the television off. "I'll be back in a minute."

A minute passed, then two, then three. He finally returned with a cold wrap used for sports injuries and a jar of something she didn't recognize. She flinched when he sat beside her on the couch, but quickly recovered.

"Give me the hand you were writing with."

Grace extended the hand to him with only a little hesitation, and he opened the jar. The room filled with the sweetest fragrance, and if she closed her eyes she could almost believe she was in a lush garden.

"The native people make this salve from a rare flower known for its healing qualities. We use it for muscle and joint pain, and also sometimes for wounds."

Asher took some of the cream and spread it onto her hand, massaging each finger individually. She let out an involuntary sigh as he used the salve and the massage to soothe the pain. It seemed to go on forever, and she didn't want him to stop.

There was a part of her brain that knew she'd only been in his care a day and that it was still far from safe to believe he was good, but another part—the part that existed only on primal feelings and urges, not logic— hoped he'd soon touch other places like that.

Then there was the orgasm from earlier that morning. How fucked up was it that she wanted him to do that again, and she wanted to return the favor? *Wrong.*

Wrong. Wrong. Wrong. The chant started up in her head again.

"Grace, are you all right?"

She looked up to see those intense, concerned blue eyes drinking her in. Asher wasn't empty. His eyes didn't pretend. Did they? She couldn't be sure. How stupid was she going to be, trusting a fantasy again? She hadn't been careful enough with Lucas. Everything had looked so good on the outside, then reality had come crashing down. No, it was too soon to be so stupid again. It would always be too soon.

But the word in her brain changed. Now it was Asher's voice in her head. *Grace. Grace. Grace. Grace.* That word that finally meant something again: Mercy. Favor. Goodwill. Could those things actually be coming from this man? If they were, she wanted to kneel at his feet and never get up.

"Grace?"

"I'm sorry, Master. I was thinking."

"Tell me." He'd finally stopped rubbing her hand and wrapped it in the cold pack, taking the fabric strap with the Velcro tab and firmly attaching it in place.

She hesitated. *Stupid. Stupid. Don't tell him anything. Don't tell him the truth. Don't be stupid again. Never trust another man. Never.* But she couldn't listen to the voice in her head, not with him so close, his very presence and touch and look compelling her to obey. She no longer knew how not to obey when an order was delivered. She'd stupidly do whatever he wanted.

"Same things," she whispered. "Afraid it's not real. This is all . . . a lot."

"I understand. I'd wanted to let you be outside some this afternoon to get used to the sunlight again. You're so pale."

She looked down at her hands, wondering if he found the pallor of her skin repulsive. She wanted to know if he wanted her outside so she could be healthy and glow, or for his own personal aesthetic. In the end, it didn't really matter. She should be grateful to go outside. Her gaze traveled behind the sofa and through the glass doors. The sun was setting.

"Have you been on the balcony yet?"

She shook her head.

"Come. I want to show you." He took her unwrapped hand and led her through the double doors. The balcony was much larger than it appeared from inside her room. There was only one lounger and a table, but there was room for much more. It was as if he was sending her a message that this was a private spot for her.

The railing came up just over her waist, and she gripped it as the island breeze ruffled her hair. They were right on the ocean. She could both hear and see the waves lapping the shore as the sun seemed to slowly sink beneath the water.

"It's lovely." She still held back, reserving her excitement for weeks or months from now, if things stayed this way.

"It's real," he whispered in her ear, the rich baritone of his voice like a song. Asher ran his fingertips through her hair, and she leaned into him without thinking. "I love this hair," he murmured.

She flushed at the compliment, glad there was something he found appealing. It was hard to see herself as more than a piece of broken trash that had been thrown out. What could she give him in return for all of this?

He unwrapped her hand. "How does it feel?"

"A little better. Thank you, Master. You didn't have to . . ."

"I take care of what's mine." He was so fierce about it that it stole any reply she might have had.

If it was real, he was going to so much trouble for her, that to show any trace of doubt in him seemed like the highest betrayal. So she kept it inside.

"Go put some shoes on. I want to show you something while there's still enough light to see it."

He let go of her hand and she went to the closet and slipped sandals on, then he took her down to the garden. It was tucked away next to the house, where the grass still grew before sloping into sandy beach.

"I thought you could take over some of the gardening. William can teach you. It'll get you outside in the sun more. I want to start you off gradually. Just a few minutes a day until your skin gets used to it."

She'd expected a lavish and well-manicured garden as lush and perfect as the rest of the house, but there were piles of perfectly good uprooted flowers and lots of dirt. Had he not liked the flowers William planted?

"It's time to move on," he said.

Looking from the pained expression on his face to the uprooted garden, she guessed it was about the other slave. Had it been a garden for her? Too many memories, maybe?

"Have you ever done any gardening?"

"No, Master."

"William still has to clear all this away and add some nutrients to the soil, but in a few days it should be ready. We can get you some books so you can decide what types of flowers you want. I'll mark everything we can get and grow here."

She searched his eyes for hints of dishonesty, but it still seemed real. It still felt like he meant all of this. The idea of working outside with a gentle breeze and the salt air and sound of the waves was so much freedom, so much more than she thought she'd ever get to taste again.

SEVEN

G race tried to get comfortable, but she couldn't. The cold, damp stone of the cell made it impossible, and the holes in the blanket kept her from being able to get warm. The faucet over by the wall wouldn't stop its incessant prattle. Drip. Drip. Drip. The dog whined and scratched at the cell door. She could hear him sniffing from behind the thick, weathered wood. Her blood ran cold.

Not again.

The door opened and Lucas stood there with an evil gleam in his eyes as the dog started sniffing his way over to her like a bloodhound. Then he was trying to get at her naked skin with his tongue through the holes in the blanket. It wasn't the dog's fault. Lucas had trained him that way.

Her master just laughed. She'd long ago stopped seeing Lucas as handsome. The permanent coldness in his dark eyes made it impossible to remember what she'd found attractive about him at all.

His features had a statuesque perfection, and that was what he reminded her of. A statue. Cold, emotionless marble that she was incapable of moving toward a humane action with even her most desperate pleas or cries for mercy. He moved with purpose, his heavy shoes thudding over the stone.

Then hands were on her, shaking her. "Wake up."

The nonsensical words coming out of his mouth, and the even more nonsensical concern in his tone, jolted her out of the dream. Grace looked frantically around her, but she wasn't in the dungeon. She was in Asher's bedroom. In Asher's bed. The bedside lamp was on.

For one terrifying slice of time, she'd thought Asher had been the dream, that she'd woken there, returned back to her real reality. But it had only been a nightmare.

She remembered now how she'd gotten here. After the garden and walking down to the ocean, they'd had dinner on the terrace. When it was time for bed, she'd gone to her room, thinking she'd sleep on the sofa, but he'd guided her to his room instead.

"You sleep with me," he'd said, his tone possessive.

So that was why she hadn't had a bed. She should have thought of that option, but the idea he'd actually allow his slave to share his bed had seemed so ludicrous, she hadn't seriously entertained it. The thrill and novelty of sleeping in a bed with her new master, of this being the permanent plan, had been almost more than she could process. But he hadn't moved to touch her, and she'd drifted into a troubled sleep, worried she'd said or done something wrong, that he was somehow displeased with her. Those fears had translated into other, more awful things in sleep. Even though he swore he'd never return her to Lucas, the fear still lingered that she might prove a large enough disappointment in the end to get taken back.

"Grace, are you all right? Your cries woke me." In the darkness she couldn't see his face to gauge if he was angry or irritated with her for waking him.

"This . . . I . . . I'm sorry. Please, I'm sorry." Having just come out of the nightmare, she was still on the defensive. She held her hands up protectively, though she knew it was a weak and pointless attempt.

He gathered her in his arms. "Shhhh. You can't help what you do in your sleep." Then he chuckled. "Though if you make it a habit to hit me at night while pretending you were dreaming, we'll have an issue."

Her hand flew to her mouth. "I . . . I hit you?"

"You've got quite a right hook."

She flinched and tried to pull away.

"Stop struggling, kitten." His voice was low, the tone she was starting to think of as his *master voice*, the tone that meant business and instantly brought her compliance. She went slack in his arms, listening to her heart still pounding too fast in her chest, as if *it* were claustrophobic right now, too.

His hand went to her hair, petting her as if she actually were a kitten. "Was the nightmare about Lucas?"

"Yes, Master."

He cursed.

"Please don't make me tell you. It was bad enough dreaming it."

He'd pulled her down next to him, pressing his warm body against hers, spooning her. His erection pressed against her back.

A terrifying thought stole into her mind. Surely if he were decent, if he were the good master she'd invented in her head, he wouldn't have a hard-on right now. Even if he'd woken with one, seeing her in so much pain and distress should have made him go limp. Shouldn't it? She shuddered against him, and then she asked the question out loud, afraid to hear the answer, and equally afraid she'd be punished for asking it, but unable to stop herself.

"Does my fear turn you on?"

His mouth was next to her ear, his voice a low growl. "It does. That scares you more, doesn't it?"

The only answer she could manage was a whimper.

"Don't worry. That's not the only thing about you that turns me on. Your delicate features and long golden hair turn me on. Feeling your naked body pressed against mine turns me on. Your vulnerability. Your desperation to please me. Your quick obedience. Your gratitude for the things I give you. You don't have to worry your fear is my only trigger. It isn't."

But it is *a trigger,* she thought, trying not to hyper-ventilate in his embrace.

Her question seemed to have only aroused him more. She tensed for a moment when his mouth found the pulse in her throat and he started to suck and nibble on the tender flesh there.

"We can deny what we are, but it won't go away. No matter what happens, your body responds to what it responds to. As does mine."

He wasn't wrong. If her fear turned him on, maybe, as wrong as it was, it turned her on a little as well, because her body was begging for his to come fill her. Her moisture was dripping out of her, and with the way they were cuddled and wrapped together, she knew in a few moments he would know as well.

Asher's hand moved around the front of her, dipping between her legs. Without conscious thought, she opened for him, giving him the access to her body that he wanted.

"You and I are both going to come tonight. I'm going to be kind. You can decide whether it's mouths, hands, toys, or my cock inside you that gets the job done."

She bit her lip as his fingers continued to massage and rub the folds of her sex, avoiding her clit until he was ready to give her more. She tried to think. Even though her body wanted him, everything was scary right now. But hands, they'd been there already. At least for her.

"Hands," she whispered. He was silent for a moment, and immediately she regretted the choice. Maybe he was disappointed in her and had expected some greater effort on her part. Something more imaginative. But surely he must understand, even being able to stand being touched by anyone was a huge feat, given that twenty-four hours ago she'd still been living the nightmare with Lucas.

"Fortune favors the brave, my dear. I suppose you'll have to wait to learn what my tongue can do."

She shivered at his words. He *was* disappointed. Well, what did he expect? Did he really expect her to be excited and eager after what she'd been through? She was grateful to him and wanted to please him, but too much of her was at war. She was afraid she'd never be able to fully give him what he wanted. And she really did want to give him everything. Between Lucas and her lingering fears about Asher and what kind of temper he might unleash on her, she just froze up.

He stopped touching between her legs when she went stiff. His hand instead went to stroking her belly. "Grace, listen to me. I know you're scared. You don't have to feel any particular thing about any of this. So stop fighting with yourself. All of this is out of your control. I am taking what's mine, but you can keep your heart. For now. You don't have to give me everything, just your body. When your body trusts me, your mind will follow. Now, open."

When his hand had moved away from her pussy, she'd closed her legs back together, as if in doing so she could protect those parts of herself from further exploration. Now, on his command, she opened them again, her body even more excited than before, and her brain more confused and upset by that fact. But he wasn't asking for her brain, just the part that had betrayed her in its willingness to comply.

She thought about all those times she'd wanted to separate and hover above while Lucas did the things he did, and now she wished she could do it for a different reason. She was scared of feeling too much pleasure with Asher, in coming to count on it and believe in it. She knew he was right. Once her body belonged fully to him, her soul, heart, mind . . . they would obediently follow behind like little soldiers. And what if it was a bad choice again? But she didn't have a choice here. He'd spelled that out clearly. Whatever happened, it wouldn't be her fault.

She hadn't hopped on a plane to go to Asher's home voluntarily. She'd been bought and brought here. Her choices were only to obey or be punished. It didn't make her bad if she wanted pleasure instead of pain, right? Her body lurched when two fingers tunneled inside her. She'd been so wrapped up in her thoughts and rationalizations that he'd taken her by surprise. His other hand was busy memorizing her body, running the planes of her face, over her hair, her breasts, her belly, her thighs. The fingers inside her started to pump in and out with greater intensity.

"You're so responsive. I like that."

His voice was so musical, like the pied piper leading her over a cliff. There was a time when, if she could have pictured this scene and all the horror of the past few months, she would have imagined fighting back, not just giving in like this. What he was doing to her body, however, felt *so* good. After feeling so bad for so long, she greedily lapped up the pleasure that was on offer. Never had a tactical invasion of fingers felt so comforting and welcome, and never had a sexual advance created so much turmoil and confusion.

"This body knows who your master is," he growled in her ear, which only made her wetter. He sat in front of her, the fingers of one hand still moving inside her while the palm of his other pressed against her clit, grinding against the swollen bit of flesh that was so hungry to be touched, harder, faster, forever.

"Be a good little slut and come for me now."

That word. *Slut.* It should have killed her response, but rolling off his tongue, the word only excited her more. It wasn't abuse. It was endearment. Though she was still afraid, he was taking control of her and taking away bits of uncertainty with each small demand. She fell back into the pattern she'd learned over eight months. Obedience without thought. Her body opened further to him, her cunt clenching around his fingers as she came.

She was panting, trying to come back to earth when his voice once again pierced the silence of the room. "Good girl. Now return the favor."

Asher's cock was the hardest she'd seen it. His hand moved possessively around the back of her neck, forcing her head up so her eyes met his. "You see, your fear isn't the only thing that makes me hard. Touch me."

Her tongue darted out to slide over her lower lip in an unconscious, nervous gesture. She reached tentatively to stroke the soft flesh, not at all sure about hands. Lucas had used her cunt, her mouth, and her ass, but he'd never had the patience for hand jobs. She wasn't sure if she was bad at it, or if he just hadn't liked them in general. But now she was paranoid it was the former.

She leaned forward, her hair falling across him as her mouth got closer to his cock.

"Now, kitten, let's not change the rules of the game midstream. That's very unfair. You said hands. I followed the rules. So will you."

Her eyes shot up to his, afraid to see anger, but instead finding mirth. She let out the breath she'd been holding and wrapped her hand around him and started pumping. *Don't be so stupid. You've given a hand job before.*

Asher leaned against the pillows and let out a hiss. "Exactly like that. Harder."

He seemed so close already that she didn't bother teasing, afraid he'd find it more annoying than pleasurable right now. A few minutes later he released over her hand and his stomach. She stared at it for a moment, unsure.

"Well? What do kittens do with cream?"

Her eyes widened for a split second before she licked her hand clean. Then she turned her attention to his belly and lapped up the warm, salty liquid from his toned stomach. He stroked her hair while she ran her tongue over him.

When she'd finished, he flicked the lamp off and went back to petting her hair as he held her against his chest. "Go back to sleep now."

Within minutes she drifted off. The rest of the night, her dreams were unmolested by Lucas and instead filled with her master's voice and hands. And images of playing kittens.

Asher woke to find Grace still lying across him, just as she'd been the night before. He'd assumed they both would have tossed and turned in their sleep, but if they had, they'd ended up together again by morning. Her hair splayed across him, and he found himself wanting to run his fingers through it again, but he resisted the urge. She looked so peaceful, he didn't want to wake her.

He carefully shifted her to the pillows and put a robe on, then slipped from the room. When he reached the kitchen, William had already started breakfast. The butler glared up at him.

"Oh, God, William. Are we back to that again? I thought we'd had this discussion."

William turned away and went back to scrambling the eggs and flipping the bacon. "Will Grace be dining with us?"

"She's still sleeping. And she won't be eating at the table. I'm starting her training today."

The butler started scrambling the eggs more vigorously. Finally, his ability to hold his tongue broke. "With all due respect, sir, I don't believe it's wise to train her like Darcy."

"Why not?"

"Treating her like an animal after what she's been through is just—"

"Stop right there. You say it like I'm going to keep her chained up and in a little crate. She's going to be treated more like a beloved pet. And it won't be all the time, anyway. Not like I'm going to make her meow or never let her do human things. She's going to garden and cook. Do cats do those things? Besides, I'm curious to see how this will go. With Darcy it was all a game. A fun game, most definitely, but Grace brings a different . . . flavor to things."

William scraped the eggs onto the plate, added bacon, and poured a glass of juice. He placed the food on the table and left the room, his final opinion on the matter delivered without words. Asher sighed. William had always been so loyal, and now it was a constant struggle with him. Apparently this house couldn't be run without at least one mouthy brat in it.

His cock twitched in his pants as he thought about Grace lying in his bed upstairs. His frightened little kitten. He was still appalled by the things Lucas had done to her, and yet the resulting effect was nothing less than spectacular.

He tried to ignore the voice in his head that told him he never could have trained a woman to be this way himself. He wasn't a hard enough master, although he found himself being more firm with Grace. She called something deep inside him that even he hadn't been aware of. He'd always known his own nature, but the nuance his newest slave called forth was at times both baffling and scary.

It was hard not to compare the two women. They were so different. One dark. One fair. One playful and disrespectful, the other so utterly broken that it caused both his chest and his pants to tighten for contradictory reasons.

Each time he found a way in which Darcy was lacking but Grace excelled, he felt guiltier. As if he were betraying his former pet's memory. He'd loved Darcy. More than life. Yet Grace stirred him out of his preoccupations with the past.

He finished his breakfast and made a list of exactly what he wanted to do with his pet for the day. Her first day had gone better than he'd expected. He'd decided being weak with her would be a greater mistake than being weak with Darcy had been. He was sure at least this time it wouldn't end in anyone's death.

Asher let her sleep for a couple more hours then climbed the stairs, wondering where she was. He found her in his bed, sitting against the headboard.

"How long have you been awake?"

"An hour," she said. She'd wrapped herself in the blankets, shielding her nudity.

"Aren't you hungry?"

"Yes, Master."

It hurt his heart to think she'd been sitting in his room, scared to leave or do anything without direct permission. If he'd just left her to come downstairs when she felt like it, she might have spent the whole day in the room. Though at some point William or he would have sought her out and at least fed her.

"You're allowed to leave this room, kitten. No one is locking you in. You need to stay on the property so someone doesn't try to run off with you, but you can go outside and down to the beach or the garden. And in a few days I'll take you out somewhere."

She tensed at that, and he remembered. The only times she'd been out with her former master had been when he'd paraded her around naked at those showings or when he just wanted to go to a club and show her off.

Asher opened the drawer in the bedside table and retrieved a platinum collar. The collar had *Property of Asher Collins* engraved in heavy block letters around it. He locked it around her throat.

Grace sat perfectly still, barely breathing as he slipped the collar around her neck and the lock clicked into place. She'd caught a glimpse of the engraved letters. She'd never had a real collar before. She hadn't known she was missing something until she'd seen other slaves wearing them when Lucas took her out. Sometimes he'd put a collar on her simply so he could attach a leash, but it had been black leather and buckled in place. It didn't lock. Not like this one.

Other girls had platinum bands locked around their throats, and Grace had felt somehow that, right or wrong, not having one of those platinum bands with her owner's name engraved on it was some sort of mark of shame, telling the world she was bad. As if Lucas didn't want to truly lay claim to her and didn't want others to know who she belonged to.

That desire had been mutual. She had never been proud to be owned by Lucas. She'd mostly just been afraid and hoping for it to somehow end, but still, she'd looked at those other slaves with their expensive collars and she felt they must have something better. Something she didn't have and would never have.

Now one of those collars was locked securely around her neck with Asher's name on it. Her fingers moved tentatively to run over the smooth metal and engraved lettering. "Thank you, Master."

"I should have put it on you yesterday, but there were so many other things going on. Would you like to talk to your friend before breakfast?"

She looked up at him. Did he mean Lainey?

"The one you spoke with yesterday on the computer."

Grace wasn't sure if she wanted to talk to Lainey or not. She felt bad that her friend had worried and mourned, but all further communication would bring were questions and more questions. Questions she didn't want to answer now. Or ever. Like what Lucas had done to her. And questions she didn't yet know how to answer. Like was Asher good to her.

He was good to her right now, but it had only been twenty-four hours. She couldn't bring herself to be that stupid, naïve girl again. Yet, at the same time, she wanted to lap up every good thing he gave her in case it all disappeared.

She flushed, thinking of the night before, waking from the nightmare and then what had happened after. Her pussy ached as she thought about his hands and what they could make her feel. How they could help her lose herself.

"Grace, I asked you a question. Would you like to speak with Lainey?"

She shook her head. "No, Master."

"Why not?"

"Too many questions."

He nodded with an understanding look on his face, and she thought the matter was dropped. But it wasn't. He pulled out his phone. "I want you to call her. What's the number?"

Grace shook her head furiously, tears welling in her eyes. "Please don't make me call her. I can't. Please . . . I don't want to . . ."

"This house is not a democracy. What's the number?"

She recited the numbers, resenting him as each word passed through her lips. Why was he doing this to her? If he was really good and she wanted space and to be left alone, then why . . .

His eyes narrowed as if he could read the thoughts playing through her mind. "After you get through, we're going to talk. Here, it's ringing." He passed the phone to her.

"Hello?"

"Hi, Lainey?"

"Grace! Is that really you?" Her friend practically shrieked over the phone. "I wasn't totally sure it was you on the computer. I mean he could have had your account information and logged on for some reason and . . ."

Grace just listened as the babbling on the other end of the phone continued, the tears streaming down her face.

"Grace?"

"Yeah?"

"Are you really okay? I don't like that you're there."

"Just stop. Please. Jesus. I've been through hell and here you are babbling on and on. I know it was hard on you, but shit. It was harder on me. You have no idea what I've been through. You'll never know or be able to understand. Talking to you is like talking to a stranger."

"Then why the fuck did you call?"

"He made me." She looked up to see Asher leaning against the wall, his arms crossed over his chest, not looking happy at all. She closed the phone, unable to take it any longer. His glare on her and Lainey's voice in her ear. She just wanted to go into a dark, quiet, place. Even Lucas's dungeon—without him in it—seemed better than this, where there was too much attention and too many demands.

Asher pushed himself off the wall and came toward her. Immediately instinct kicked in and she dropped to her knees in front of him.

"Why did you hang up on her?"

"Please, Master. This slave . . . she can't . . . she can't . . ." *So stupid. Why did I do that?* It was just a phone call. It wasn't one of the hundreds of awful things Lucas had done to her. How could she have been so stupid? And now what? From the anger radiating off him, she just knew his mercy was at an end. How could she allow herself to disappoint him so much in the space of only a day?

He must be regretting buying her. That thought made the bottom of her stomach drop out. He'd been so . . . decent to her. And she was throwing tantrums? It was just too much. Surely he must understand. If he knew what she'd been through, even a little of it, he had to understand. But she'd never done this shit with Lucas. Not once. She was too terrified of him to do anything but beg and obey. Somehow Asher deserved less than Lucas now?

"Don't move." He left and she stayed where she was, imagining all the horrible things that could happen next. If it had been Lucas, her thoughts would have been only about what she would have to endure. But with Asher, the biggest thought on her mind was how she'd disappointed him. And how much she wanted to obey. He returned several minutes later.

"Master, I'm sorry. I'm trying. I'm a bad slave, you must be so disappointed. I don't know why I can't . . ."

"Shhh." He sat on the floor beside her and lifted her chin. "Sit up. I want you to eat something." He gave her a banana and a hard-boiled egg that must have been sitting in the fridge overnight. And some juice.

"I don't deserve . . . "

"I take care of what's mine. Remember? I'm not having you missing meals. You'll get sick. Eat." When she started to eat, he got up and crossed the hall to her room. She looked up when he came back to see he had a brush in his hand. Grace couldn't stop the little shudder, as if he might beat her with it. Instead he sat behind her and brushed her hair while she ate.

"I understand this is all hard for you. Whatever I tell you to do, I expect you to do. I will punish you, and eventually punishments will involve a cane. But not today. Don't try my patience, Grace. I won't ever allow myself to be weak with you. If you start to view my mercy as weakness, then we're going to have a serious problem. And I don't want to cause you further damage, do you understand?"

"Yes, Master." Every time he said something like this she just felt worse. Like such an ingrate. If this was real . . . if she could manage not to do anything to sway him away from the way he was being with her, she owed him everything. And she was disobeying him left and right already.

"I know I'm pushing hard with your friend, but I want you to have your friendship back. I insist on it."

By this time she'd finished her breakfast and he'd stopped brushing. "Go stand in the corner."

He helped her to her feet and she moved to where he'd pointed, fighting the tremble in her body as she went, wondering what was coming next. She stood, tensed for a few minutes, waiting for . . . something. But whatever she'd thought was coming never arrived.

"Don't move from that spot. I want you to spend this time thinking. I'll come get you when it's time for lunch. We'll talk further about the rules in this house at that time."

EIGHT

Asher descended the stairs, clicking the most recently dialed number on his cell as he went. "Hello?" a guarded voice answered.

"Is this Lainey?"

"Yes, who is this?" But she knew. He could tell from her voice that she knew.

"This is Asher. Grace is with me."

A long silence. When she spoke, her voice cracked. "Please let her go. She needs to come home where she'll be safe."

He sighed. "I need you to listen to me, Lainey. The things she's been through . . . you don't just *recover* from them. Do you understand what I'm telling you?"

There was more silence, except for the sound of soft crying. Perhaps he was justifying keeping what he wanted, what he'd paid so much money to acquire.

No. He was right. Even the way she'd reacted to calling Lainey, like he was somehow punishing her by trying to get her to speak to someone who loved her. She couldn't live in that world. Not anymore. But he could give her a small piece of it.

"I need you to do me a favor."

"Why would I do anything to help you?" Her voice was like acid.

"It's for Grace. I'm not the one who hurt her."

"But you're the one keeping her now."

He sighed. "I'm not going to debate this with you. You can think I'm the bad guy all you want. There is nothing you can do to alter the course of her life. What you *can* do is help her by doing what I say. I want her to be able to maintain a friendship, so I need you to agree to not bring up anything about her current or past situation on the island. It's too upsetting for her. If she chooses to talk about it, let her come to you. Can you do that for me?"

"Fine. But I don't like you."

He chuckled. "I can't imagine what you must feel about Lucas, then. And Lainey?"

"What?"

"Thank you."

He stared at the phone, unsure why it mattered so much to him that Grace be able to connect with this friend. It made her so uncomfortable.

Even so, he couldn't let her erase it all. He wanted to give her every chance possible to heal as much as she could. Rekindling a close friendship seemed like a step in that direction.

A few hours later he returned to the bedroom to find Grace standing naked in the corner, just as he'd left her. His cock hardened at the sight of her so delicate and vulnerable. He'd made sure to keep his footfalls silent when he'd come back, to see if she was where she was supposed to be, not trying to cheat or squirm out of the punishment. She hadn't moved an inch.

"Kitten?"

She looked up, her eyes red, her lower lip trembling. It made him want to shove her against the wall and fuck her right then. It was so wrong that her tears turned him on.

"Yes, Master?"

"Are you going to continue to show me attitude?"

"No, Master."

He knew it wasn't the punishment that drove her. It wasn't the idea of standing for hours in a corner like some recalcitrant child. She was ashamed she'd displeased him. It genuinely upset her. When she looked at him, he could see how much she wanted to give to him and how afraid she still was that he might be toying with her. He was surprised she was already as willing as she was to please and obey, but she'd latched onto him as her savior, as her god. And every second standing in her presence made him want to step more firmly into that role.

It obviously weighed on her, her two minor bits of disobedience. With Darcy, he wouldn't have worked up to punishment for such minor issues. It wouldn't have been worth the hassle. Right or wrong, though, he couldn't stand to let Grace get away with even the smallest infraction. He wanted everything from her. Every tiny corner in her mind and in her heart he wanted as his own personal real estate. He wanted not the slightest bit of hesitance when he issued a command. He wanted her to be willing, grateful, subservient putty in his hands. And he was quickly running out of motivation to feel guilt for that.

He handed her the cell phone. "Call Lainey again."

A flicker of something passed over her face. Not defiance. Resignation. Good. She was already resolving to be his good girl.

She took the phone from him and dialed. The call started tentatively, but within a few moments they were edging around the circumstances of Grace's life to talk about other things, catching up on what Lainey had been up to. He was thankful the friend was listening to him and not letting her personal feelings get in the way of Grace's own good.

He made the bed, smiling when she lost herself for a moment and gushed about her room and the balcony and the view. Already she sounded somewhat like a person. For all Lucas had done to her, he hadn't left her an empty shell yet. She was still in there somewhere, with wants and desires and dreams that had been cast aside in favor of survival.

Several minutes later she shyly handed the phone to him, brushing a stray strand of hair behind her shoulder. "Thank you, Master."

He slipped the cell into his pocket and pulled her flush against him, not giving her time to react or process. Then his fingers were inside her. He let out a satisfied chuckle at how wet she was for him, how desperately her body sought completion with his, even if her mind was still quite terrified. His mouth moved to the shell of her ear.

"I plan to be inside you, *very* soon," he practically growled at her.

Her answering whimper drew his eyes to hers. He could see the conflicting emotions flitting over her face, the edges of lust trying to overtake the fear, the confusion and shame over feeling anything at being treated this way. Too many negative emotions appeared to overwhelm her, until she seemed to crawl inside herself and go numb.

"Grace, stay right here with me. You aren't with him. I'm not him."

The use of her name called her back. She was still afraid, obviously. No reason she shouldn't be. He was moving the timetable of his plans for her at a warp speed that made even him dizzy. He knew it was unfair, wrong. He knew how broken and damaged she was, how traumatized.

She did something to him, something almost hypnotic. There were no words in the English language, or that of the island, to express the mad possession he felt when he was near her. The need to mark. And take. And rut like animals until they were both sweaty and sated.

He wanted her to beg him to never remove his hands from her body. And though such an outcome seemed improbable given her history, some part of him still hoped for that ending. Asher licked the side of her throat and sucked on her pulse point. It was beating wildly against his mouth like a bird trapped in a small cage, fluttering to escape.

His fingers dove back inside her at a harder and heavier pace. In his head he could hear tribal drums as if they'd been taken with a sexual possession they were both helpless to stop. In reality, she was the only helpless one in this equation, but it only made his cock harder, only made him grip her tighter.

"Grace, Grace, Grace." He chanted the word, soft and low, like a prayer in her ear, and with every repetition of her name another muscle group seemed to relax until her body was loose and receptive, waiting for him to come fill her. "Yes, that's it, kitten. You know what I want from you. Whose cunt is this?"

"Yours, Master." Her hips were bucking against him now, fucking his fingers, giving as much as he gave. It was clear she'd moved beyond cognitive thought and all the reasons she should feel shame for still wanting something so carnal. The only thing that seemed to exist was her body and what it needed from him in this moment.

"I will never use your kink against you. I will never deny you an orgasm. I don't want you to ever lose touch with your own body and pleasure again. Come for me."

She tensed as if she wasn't sure she could just come on demand like that.

"Grace . . . relax. Your body knows what it wants. Just let it obey me." As his fingers moved inside her, his thumb stroking over her clit, he felt her let go and come apart in his hands.

Grace shuddered against him as once again her body's reactions spun out of control. The pleasure seemed to go on for a quiet eternity, punctuated only by the ragged sound of her own breath. What was this man doing to her? *How can I feel this way after Lucas? What's* wrong *with me?*

The sound of a zipper pulled her out of her thoughts. He'd moved away to get his clothes off. And then he was standing there, too beautiful to be real. Her mouth went dry. Sure, Lucas had been attractive. Muscle-group to muscle-group, it would have been a hard contest. Until she moved up to faces. Whereas Lucas had black eyes like pits you could starve and die in, Asher's were like intense blue flame, eyes that softened when they looked at her in a way Lucas's never had, no matter how hard she'd tried to please him.

She carefully avoided staring at his cock, unsure if she could deal with that appendage in a positive way again. Her hand had been on it the night before, and she'd been okay enough then, but what about when he fucked her? He was thicker than Lucas. He would feel different inside, right? The self-talk was still running through her head when Asher moved her to her hands and knees on the bed.

The world narrowed to the feelings gathering below her waist. Her wetness made everything feel as if it throbbed more, blood rushing south to prepare her for what was about to happen, even as her mind struggled to catch up to what her body wanted. Her body wanted to submit to him like some bitch in heat, wanted to be spread open until his leering gaze could take in every contour of her cunt.

A shiver slid over her. *So, so wrong.* Fear warred with lust as he prodded at her opening, and then he was inside her. She panicked as memories of Lucas raping her bloomed in her mind, fresh pain lancing through her.

"No, please . . . oh God, please stop." She was whimpering, shaking, not believing he would stop, hating herself for begging him to, for being anything but endlessly grateful for the things he'd given her and the things he'd chosen not to take away.

And then he wasn't inside her anymore.

Asher moved onto the bed, cradling her in his arms, rocking her, whispering *Shhhh* in her ear. She knew her body was his to take and bizarrely wanted to give it to him. She wanted to wrap her will up in a box, shutting out all her protests and fears. She wanted to put a bow on it and lay it at his feet.

And yet.

At some point he would take her, and he wouldn't stop. If she'd kept her mouth shut and let him keep going, maybe the flashback would have passed. Now it would only be more frightening the next time he approached her like this. Until they breached this wall without her losing her mind.

What if she kept begging? What if she couldn't stop and just let him take and use and have that which he'd paid for and fed and clothed? Some wild and frenzied part of her prayed that the next time he would gag her so her protests couldn't reach him and they could get through it without the event building ever larger and scarier in her head with each failed attempt.

There was a long moment of silence. He was thinking so loud she could almost hear it. Or perhaps that was just the way of things after being held captive in a dungeon for months. You became less human, more animal. You lived on instincts, read body language. You learned to anticipate things even if sometimes you desperately wanted to remain in the dark about the next moment.

Right now, Grace knew he was contemplating his next action. Would he punish her for begging him to stop? Would he start again? Would he start handling her like a piece of fragile, blown glass? Something of beauty to keep in a curio cabinet, but never to touch.

He sighed, and she went stiff.

"I'm sorry, Master."

"For?"

His hand had gone to stroking through her hair and down her back. It was so soothing she couldn't think. Was he angry with her? He didn't sound angry. Was he disappointed? It occurred to her that the last thing she ever wanted to do was disappoint this man. And it was becoming less about the fear he'd return her to Lucas. On some basic level, she couldn't convince herself he'd do that even though they were still relative strangers to each other. Another part of her brain jumped in immediately to chastise her for being so stupid and trusting. *Didn't you learn your lesson the first time? With the last one?*

"I must be such a disappointment for you," she whispered, finally.

He stopped petting her hair and the silence seemed to suck the oxygen from the room. "Let me get this straight . . . you are tortured for months and nearly starved, then you consider it your fault when you're afraid of a complete stranger who just bought you?"

She shrugged, no longer sure what the correct answer was. She'd made a list in her head of all the times she'd already disappointed or disobeyed when she'd never before wanted this much to give something to another person in gratitude for the hell he'd taken her away from.

"Look at me," he demanded.

She raised her face to his. If she hadn't been wrapped in his arms, she would have run far away from the look in his eyes. She was still terrified to have that kind of intensity turned on her. Especially when she wasn't altogether sure what it meant yet. If it meant pain or pleasure or something in between.

His fingers played over the column of her throat above the collar whose weight was already becoming a comfort of sorts. "I believe you and I both came to this island for the same reason. We both wanted something real. I wanted something real that was legal, where I could be sure the other person came to me freely. I never saw myself as the type of man who would just take without some basic initial consent in place first. But when I saw you, the only thing I could think of was possessing you. I know what you've been through. I know I'm probably damaging you further. I should stop making excuses and release you, find someone out in the real world that can help you somehow."

He said *real world* as if they had both been caught up in some fuzzy bubble of a dream. Was this not real? And *had* he damaged her further? She couldn't think of a way he had.

She gripped his arms, clutching onto him like a life-line. "Please, don't get rid of me."

He lifted her chin. "Kitten, I don't want to be a monster with you, but I won't own you while you call the shots. No matter your history. I understand what you've been through is unimaginable, which is why I'm offering you your freedom off this island. I'm sure you would be welcome with Lainey. But if you stay, I will fuck you, and there will be no plea for mercy that will make me stop. When I said I was going to be inside you very soon, I meant it. I won't have another slave that I don't own on *every* level."

Something that had been coiled tightly inside her, feeling like a bomb about to go off, began to loosen. The vise in her chest released, and she could breathe normally again. He wasn't going to torture her with the growing dread, wondering if he would stop or if he wouldn't. She had her answer on that, at least.

Grace knew she should take the offer. But then what? If she took her chance at freedom she'd die alone and miserable. She could see no other way it could play out. In all the times she'd thought about it outside of impossible daydreams, she'd imagined being scared to leave her house, jumping at every noise, fearing every man that got near her, bile rising in her throat if one actually touched her, no matter how innocent or acci-dental the touch, never being able to have a normal rela-tionship with a man. And kink was definitely off the table.

But Asher was right. Her body responded to what it responded to. Inexplicably, all of Lucas's cruel treatment couldn't rewire her brain or make her skin stop humming when in the presence of a dominant male. No matter how scared she was.

If she went back home, she could pretend she wasn't wrong, but she knew her hand would still drift between her legs, and she'd still have the same fucked-up fantasies. And each time she brought herself off, she would die just a little more. And not a single living soul would understand her, what she felt, what she needed but could never have, what her body still wanted in spite of all the evidence she'd acquired to prove it could never work. Not in real life. Not ever.

The alternative was still holding her, waiting. She wanted him to rescind the offer because she couldn't handle this kind of responsibility again. His jaw clenched as if holding back the words that would say: *Fuck it. You're mine. You belong to me and I'll take you until you stop crying and beg me to keep going.*

God, why couldn't it have been Asher instead of Lucas the first time? Why? She was being teased with something she should have had. And if she took it now, what did that say about her? Somehow him giving her a chance at freedom was worse than not giving it because once again she was faced with the choice . . . be free or be a slave. And once again she wanted to be the latter, wanted to trust that this could be something other than a waking nightmare.

But if she made the wrong choice again . . .

Him buying her had been the one shining beacon. Whatever he did to her, she hadn't voluntarily walked into it. Those thoughts ran on a loop in her mind until finally he broke the tension, shoving past the barriers of a battle he'd been waging in his own mind. A battle she'd felt as his hands had tightened on her arms, no doubt leaving marks that would later turn to bruises.

She knew she'd stand in front of the mirror, running her fingers over the marks left by his hand, and that somehow, it wouldn't be the same as the marks Lucas had forced her to endure. They would be marks she'd touch and look at every day, becoming sadder as they faded, leaving nothing but the memory of his hands on her.

He gripped her even tighter so that she had to bite her lip not to cry out. "No," he said.

Grace was so still her breath seemed to move in and out of her more slowly and quietly, as if in stealth mode. *No, what?*

"I'm sorry. I thought I could give you the option of freedom. I know it's the right thing to do. I've only had you a day. I shouldn't be this attached. But I can't do it. It's worse that I even offered. You're never leaving here. I will never free you."

His voice was threaded with regret and pain, emotions she couldn't convince herself were the same as Lucas's Puppet Theater of Fake Feelings.

She said the only thing she could say, the only words that would move from her brain to reach her mouth. "Thank you, Master."

Asher tensed. "For?"

"For giving me the choice long enough to know I didn't want that burden anymore. And for taking it away before I had to decide." Suddenly something felt safe. He wasn't going to leave her to go through life alone and broken. He wouldn't return her to Lucas. The flashbacks would stop; eventually they would. And if they didn't? Then they wouldn't have anyway. At least now there would be someone to hold her and keep away the chill from that cold, dungeon floor.

Asher lay back on the bed, a satisfied and predatory gleam in his eyes that only made Grace fall further under his power. "Straddle me, kitten."

She followed the instruction, this time more hyper-aware of the fact that his erection was pressing against her mound and lower belly. Only this time there was no fabric standing between them. He took her hand and brought her closer to him, kissing her palm.

His words were soothing when he spoke, as if he understood she was a frightened, wild thing, and he was trying to coax her toward something she would like if only she could learn to place her trust in him. There was a promise there, and she wanted to believe in it so badly it made her ache. If only she could keep Lucas from crowding out all the good thoughts and feelings in her brain to experience one thing that was pure.

"You were okay when my fingers were inside you. This is only another part of the same body that already made you come. I perhaps shouldn't have taken you from behind the first time, where you couldn't see me. I was trying to avoid hurting your back." He looked at her expectantly, waiting for her to mount him.

He was trying to make it easier, but the look in his eyes said his cock would be inside her one way or another within the next couple of minutes, either of her own volition or against her will. She could pretend she was in control and ride him like he wanted, or he could take her the way he'd started out.

No matter how long she'd been on the island, with its strange culture and laws, there was still the part of her that saw the world in the same black and white she'd been trying to escape. The thoughts that this was wrong, that she was wrong, wouldn't stop going through her mind, even though she knew she had no hope of ever leaving this place, and no one would judge her for being a good slave.

Whatever fears she had of flashbacks and dreams that might haunt her forever, Asher was a different man, and she was his property. Her stomach fluttered at that idea, and she had to push back another redundant wave of self-recrimination. Right now, she was on top. He was giving her this to help her. And she was grateful for the small mercy.

Before he could say her name or his pet name for her in the *master voice*, she made the decision and shoved his cock inside her. In spite of everything that had happened, she was still dripping, a furnace of want and need and primal urges that refused to take the past into account. Everything was quiet then, except for the sound of their bodies sliding against one another as she raised and lowered herself on him.

"Good girl," he said, the praise sending another flip of pleasure through her. The look in his eyes was so intense that she couldn't break the contact. It was a connection that flowed between them and gave her something that felt safe to hold onto as they broke through the one wall that had scared her so much.

She'd expected he would fuck her soon enough, once she'd known she'd been bought for that purpose. But she hadn't expected some part of her to want him to.

"Grace," he hissed, closing his eyes briefly, ". . . so fucking tight. This is exactly what I want from you right now."

The eye contact and his repeated use of her name tethered her to the here and now, and though she could feel Lucas pounding on the doors of her mind, trying to slither in where he could harm her, Asher wouldn't loosen the connection enough for her to be tormented by the ghost hanging over them.

He *did* feel different. So different. His cock expanded her walls to a degree she hadn't known was possible. A few minutes of this leisurely pace went by before he lost patience with it. He gripped her waist, holding her in place as he drove into her from below. "Come again," he growled.

She did. And then he did. And suddenly she was lying on top of him, and he was panting. Then the realization hit her. He'd come inside her. So he must know what Lucas had done. It must have been in the papers he'd had on her that gave her name and her measurements, and God only knew how many other private details.

A few days into her imprisonment with Lucas, he'd brought a doctor in who had performed a procedure to make her unable to have children. She'd been sore for days afterward. Grace had never thought about having children. Such a choice didn't seem to fit into the kind of lifestyle she'd wanted. With kids, she'd have to circumscribe her life so as not to warp them. In a world without legal slavery, it would have been child abuse for them to even see an obvious collar clasped around her throat, not understanding what it meant or why it was okay for a man to treat a woman that way when the whole world said otherwise.

Her fingers strayed now to the platinum band resting securely in its place around her throat. No, she'd never thought she would want children, and yet the shock of having that choice forever revoked, of no longer having the option to feel a life growing inside her, had left her mourning for days. The memories caused tears to fall again, a few dropping onto her master's shoulder.

NINE

Asher rubbed the salve over her back, re-dressed the wounds, and then wrapped a black silk robe around her, tying it at her hip. Her gaze was unfocused. She was off in her own world, and he didn't know if he should disturb it. Had she gone to a good place or a bad place in her mind? Did she need time to process what had just taken place between them?

Although he felt guilt for pushing her so soon, he also reveled in the way her body gave in to his demands and how good she felt impaled on his cock.

He took her hand, his thumb pausing and pressing against the pulse point in her wrist. Slow and steady. He tugged on her and she stumbled forward a bit before her feet began moving.

"Grace?"

She looked up, her gaze suddenly clear. "Yes, Master?"

Such a fragile thing, as if she'd easily shatter in his hands. He found the power heady and erotic. The moment her back was healed, he had plans. "Are you ready for lunch?"

She nodded.

He guided her downstairs to the kitchen, where she glanced around as if looking for intruders. He recalled watching her at the showing, how self-conscious she was. Though she was too broken to rebel.

He intended to have her dressed in public. In something wicked and kinky, yes, but still, everything covered. Random exhibitionism didn't turn her on, and Asher didn't particularly get off on the idea of every dirty old man on Eleu assessing his property like window shoppers, either. The two of them were happily compatible in that way.

Her shoulders loosened as she realized they were alone.

"The driver stays in the pool house, and I'll ask William not to lurk so much. It's a large estate, and he can stay in the east wing. He's got his own apartment and kitchen down there."

Grace relaxed at that, but she still seemed on edge. They'd gone over a day without him laying out his most basic instructions. Once he got her into a routine, it would be better. He snapped and pointed beside the chair at the head of the table. There was a large, fluffy, round cushion on the floor. William had gotten it set up after breakfast.

"You will never stand in my presence at home. William has put out cushions around the house so you won't hurt your knees. I won't make you crawl everywhere, especially if there isn't carpet." She tentatively moved toward the cushion he'd pointed at and knelt. Peace drifted into her features as bits of structure were erected around her.

He continued. "You may roam freely around the house, but stay out of William's living area. Also, my study is off-limits unless I call for you. The dungeon is also off-limits unless I take you there." Not that he thought she had any inkling toward hanging out in the dungeon alone.

She kept her eyes down, her pose so sweetly submissive it drove him to distraction. "We already went over proper address. You'll have a few chores. Mostly just keeping your room clean, maybe a little cooking. And the garden, though I mean for that to be more of an outlet than work. If you find you don't like gardening you don't have to do it. We'll find you another hobby. Never leave the property without me. You may wear normal clothing except when I say otherwise. Other than that, just do as I say when I say it. I won't hesitate to punish you, despite your history. Are we clear?"

"Yes, Master."

Asher crossed to the cupboard and pulled out plates and glasses, busying himself with reheating a casserole William had made and left for them in the refrigerator. In his peripheral vision, he caught her watching his every move from the cushion on the floor. When both plates were heated and tea was poured, he placed his on the counter and hers on the hardwood in front of her.

"Kittens don't eat at the table. Kittens don't really get silverware either, but I'll make an exception for you." His chest tightened as he watched her tilt her head to the side as if she couldn't remember what gentle teasing felt like.

"William put a cushion in your room. If you ever want to take a nap, you can sleep on that, or your sofa, or the lounger on your balcony. You'll only sleep in the bed at night, with me. And only if you're not being punished for something." Her body grew still beside him, and he ran his fingers through her hair. She leaned against his leg.

He continued to pet her. "When we're in public—" She tensed at that. "—you won't speak unless spoken to and never to anyone besides me. In private you can always speak to me freely without asking. Just be respectful, though I know I won't have to worry about that with you. You may also, of course, talk to William if you like, and your friend, Lainey. You can ask to call and speak to her or talk to her on the computer at any time. I can set up a webcam for you if you'd like to see each other."

She seemed to be soaking it all in. He wished she felt comfortable enough to initiate conversation. Eventually they'd get there.

Grace knew she was trapped in the dream with Lucas, the dungeon, the tattered blanket, the whip. She could feel the blood running down her back far too fast to be real, and far too much to survive. Yet, survive, she did. *It's not real. It's not real. It's not real.*

Over and over the mantra repeated itself in her head. But the pounding of her pulse in her ears felt real. The fear felt real. The pain felt real. She tried to hold onto the fleeting realization that she was asleep and it would be over and she'd be safe as soon as she reached consciousness.

She was with Asher now, she had been for weeks, and she was starting to relax and trust him. Still, Lucas sometimes visited at night. The specter of her former master unwilling to let her go.

"Master, help me," she said, as if somehow Asher could hear her from outside in the real world in his bed where she was no doubt being held against him in a protective embrace. Maybe she was shouting it in her sleep. She could only hope.

Any minute now, he might wake her from the nightmare as he had so many times before. Each time he'd pulled her into his arms, stroking her back, whispering soothing nonsense. Each time, she'd feel his hardness against her. It still bothered her that her fear made him want to fuck her, but she found herself unable to fight against the sexual way he enthralled her to his will, making every orgasm sweeter than the last.

Lucas turned dark eyes on her. "Help you? Oh no, I'm just beginning. Look at all the lovely toys I have for us to play with."

Grace squeezed her eyes shut so she wouldn't have to see the table of *toys,* most of which were meant to make her scream and cry and bleed.

"I wasn't talking to you," she said with disgust. As she'd started to recognize the dreams while they were happening, she'd gotten braver. Maybe too brave.

He rushed at her then, gripping her shoulders hard and shaking her. "You filthy little cunt. You will pay for that mouth of yours."

Grace opened her eyes to find Asher shaking her. Yes, he'd heard her cry out for his protection. She wrapped her arms around him, squeezing too hard, her tears wetting his skin as she buried her head in his neck. The nightmares weren't happening as frequently anymore, but they were still happening. She marveled that he had any patience left. He must be so ready for her to just *get over it.*

She knew such feelings were irrational. He understood, but she still felt horrible dragging him through this.

At least things were better when she was awake. Though she sometimes still fought with herself over what may be foolishness, she couldn't help trusting him. Asher was so consistent, so gentle, so powerful. Every cell in her body strained to do his bidding. And each time he saved her from Lucas, Grace felt just a little more grateful, slipping further into her role.

In the few unguarded moments that crept in, she recognized herself as becoming . . . happy? The lingering, occasional nightmare was the only remaining dark cloud over them.

"Grace? Just a dream, baby. I'm here." The deep rumble of his voice was like a warm blanket wrapping her in comfort. Her body stopped shaking at the sound of it.

"I can't go back to sleep."

"I know. Come with me." Neither of them were clothed and he didn't go for the closet; he just took her hand in his, and she obediently followed him down the stairs. When they got to the study and he pulled the book halfway out of the bookcase, she shook her head.

"Please . . . don't." Why was he doing this? Was she somehow still asleep? She tried to tug her hand out of his grip. In the weeks she'd belonged to him, she'd been surprised he'd never taken her to the dungeon. Asher's dominance over her had been quiet and gentle.

Even the sex had followed that pattern. A few toys, silk scarves to tie her to the bed frame, a blindfold on occasion after he'd worked her up to it. The blindfold had been harder because she couldn't see him to remind herself it was him and not Lucas. But he'd talked to her the whole time so she wouldn't forget who she was with.

It had all been more like vanilla-kink than any of the more hardcore fantasies she'd had before coming to Eleu. And yet . . . with Lucas in her past, even the tame activities had felt reckless and scary at first. The understanding of Asher's total ownership of her and the mercy he continually showed as he eased her back into pleasure, were things she'd started to take for granted.

And now it seemed it was over. She hated herself for even trying to fight him. He'd been so good to her. So kind. And she thought she had the right to question him or resist? She should be willing to give him anything in return for what he'd taken her out of. No matter what he did, it was unlikely to be as bad as Lucas. She looked up into his eyes, horrified by the disappointment shining out at her.

"I'm sorry, Master. The nightmares, I can't . . . please . . . please take me back upstairs." She'd hit the panic point. The trembling, the crying. And yet his erection hadn't flagged. Her safety was about to shatter. This was the moment. This was why that part of her mind had chided her for being so trusting. She'd always known it would end, that they'd be here and the nightmare would be back, no longer just when she was sleeping.

She was quickly losing the ability to breathe right, barreling toward hyperventilation at an alarming speed.

"Grace, look at me."

Even the utterance of her name couldn't call her out of the downward spiral of fear.

"Who do you belong to?" he said, his voice taking on that edge, the one that said he was serious and she'd better listen up. He turned the dial on the heater to warm the room.

She took a shuddering breath. "You, Master," she whispered.

"It's time to introduce you to pain."

Grace closed her eyes. She had to be dreaming still. She'd already been formally introduced to pain and didn't want to become reacquainted. How could he do this to her? *Why* would he do this to her? Especially when she was still fresh from a nightmare. She wanted to lash out, ask questions, accuse, but all she could do was beg.

"Master, please . . . please don't do this to me. You know I can't take it. You know what I've been through."

"Your nightmares won't ever be purged until we do this. Until you know what this will be like with me. You've known it was coming for a long time. And I told you from the beginning I would do exactly what I wanted with you, that I would have you whenever and however it pleased me."

She wanted to ask where he got his logic about purging her nightmares. Some pseudo-psychology text-book? "Why do you want to hurt me? I don't under-stand." *So stupid, Grace. Trusting him was so fucking stupid.*

"Kitten, do you know the difference between hurt and harm?"

She just stared at him. Because she knew if she opened her mouth she'd lash out. Suddenly she wanted to break free and run from the house. She fantasized about stealing his boat and just drifting off to sea. Why hadn't she done it before now? She'd had the opportun-ity. But she'd stayed like a battered wife. Though she hadn't been battered by Asher, she still didn't seem to have the self-preservation instincts of a pea.

Why hadn't she taken the chance at freedom before he'd changed his mind? If she'd spoken quickly enough when he'd made the offer, would he have felt enough pity to follow through rather than taking it back? She'd never know.

"Answer me. That wasn't rhetorical."

She wanted to say she knew the difference, but she wasn't sure she knew his definitions or even if she could separate things out that much in her head anymore, so she said, "No, Master."

He helped her down the steps into the dungeon, then pointed at the ground where he or William must have set out another cushion. It was hard to go where he'd directed because she'd feel even more vulnerable kneel-ing. But she moved to where he wanted her.

Asher leaned against the spanking horse, his arms crossed over his chest. "Grace, I *will* hurt you—"

She cringed at that. To hear him state it so bluntly and without apology caused the rest of her faith to crumble. She never should have trusted him. Not for a single minute. He held all the power. Of course he would use it against her. She'd always known it.

"—but I will never harm you. I will never leave permanent scars on you. I'll never make you bleed. I'll never leave you with internal injuries or broken bones. I'll never torture you or give you more than I know you can handle. Pain will either ultimately be for mutual pleasure or for discipline, but even as discipline it isn't something you should fear from me. Not the way you're fearing it."

She'd known that punishments like writing lines and standing in a corner wouldn't last and she'd done her best not to break rules or disobey or displease him. When she did, the punishment was immediate. But it hadn't been physical pain, so far.

"Why can't it just be for punishment?" She was already making vows and promises in her head to never displease him enough to warrant physical punishment. If she could get him to agree to restrict the pain to punishment, maybe she could find some way to be perfect and never mess up, to never have to feel the sting of the whip or anything else ever again.

"Because I like it." His gaze was level on her when he said it.

Despair at the hopelessness of the situation caused the tears to finally start sliding down her cheeks. "But what about me?"

He pushed himself off the spanking horse and moved a few steps toward her, until he was within touching distance. "What about you? I care for you. I protect you. I provide for you. But never forget that you are mine.

The choices I make for you are made with your ultimate well-being in mind, but also with my desires in mind."

She didn't say anything, just looked at the stone floor and his bare feet.

"Kitten, what happens in the dreams now?"

She'd told him all this before, why did he want to hear it again? Why was he tormenting her? "He makes me hurt. He hits me."

"Is that all he does?"

"Yes."

"And what did he do before in the dreams . . . when you first had them?"

"Please . . . "

"Tell me," Asher demanded.

"You already know."

"And I want to hear it again."

"He hurt me, and raped me, and let the dog . . . " she trailed off, unable to complete the sentence.

"But now he just physically hurts you?"

"Yes, Master."

He sat beside her and pulled her against his chest. She sagged into his warmth, even though she didn't want to. He'd become as frightening to her again as he'd been the first day when he'd taken her out of Lucas's dungeon. When she'd thought she'd die at his hands.

"Grace, I don't think these nightmares are just about Lucas. I think it's about your lingering fear of what might happen with me. The fear that you aren't really safe yet. Once we got through the sex, and you started trusting me there, that aspect of the nightmares disappeared. We have to do pain now so we can kill him off completely. Trust me."

She wanted to, but she couldn't. It was asking far too much. Even if years passed in his care it would be asking too much. Part of her wanted to do whatever he wanted, but she wasn't sure if she could make herself willingly accept what was about to happen. And then what? Would it turn into a punishment? Wouldn't that be worse?

He stood and pulled her to her feet. "Come on, be a good girl for me."

"What if I have a flashback?"

"We'll work through it and go slow. Believe me, it will be different. You'll know exactly who you're with."

He had to half drag her to the spanking horse anyway; she just couldn't make her feet move and was grateful he seemed to understand. "Straddle it, kitten, and lie on your stomach for me."

She mounted the black, vinyl-padded bench, and Asher adjusted the section her knees would rest on. The part she straddled and lay across was long and not too wide, so that her breasts pressed over the sides. She tensed when he strapped her ankles and wrists to the lower bench.

"Shhhh," he said, his hand running the length of her back and dipping between the cleft of her ass. "It's for your safety, so you don't inadvertently struggle and hurt yourself."

The bench pressed tight against her mound, quickly warming from her body heat. He pressed a button and vibrations started. She let out a surprised moan. No spanking horse she'd ever been on, before the island and after, had ever vibrated. She pressed harder against the vinyl.

He chuckled. "I have attachments for penetration, but let's not overwhelm you today." She shivered. "Is that a good shiver or a bad shiver?"

It made her feel bizarrely safe that he noticed everything about her. Each nuance of expression, each tremble, each goose bump that popped out over her flesh in response to him. At least he was aware of what was going on, which meant anything delivered by him would be deliberate.

"Good shiver, Master," she said, blushing. Already he was making her forget her anxiety, and she was almost back to thinking maybe she could trust him. Though Asher was demanding and insistent and never treated her like glass or like she was a *special case* to him, she'd somehow been okay.

Perhaps it was the utter helplessness of her situation. With no hope of ever gaining her freedom and a master who didn't seem intent on harming her, her brain had moved quickly into Stockholm mode and along the path to acceptance. Somehow she was able to tolerate and even love his touch: his hands, tongue, and cock on her and inside her.

Her submissive instincts had answered his every demand, as if the two of them together created a perfectly choreographed dance. Of course he would make this tolerable as well. But then, the hitting hadn't started yet, so maybe it was a little soon to be making those kinds of judgments.

Her head turned toward the sound of the trunk opening. He seemed to be getting lots of things. Bad shiver. A few tears slipped out along with a little whimper.

"Grace—I haven't even touched you yet."

He began methodically placing objects on the table: a flogger, a riding crop, a paddle, a cane. She shut her eyes, unable to deal with a table laid out so much like the one in the dream.

"Please . . . " She didn't know what else to put with that sentence, so she just dropped her head back onto the bench. Her begging wouldn't sway him. The time she'd spent with him had already proven that. If Asher said something was going to happen, it was going to happen. And it was going to happen on his timetable. Very often that certainty brought a measure of comfort and safety. But not this time.

He came to stand beside her, his hand resting on the small of her back. The light pressure and warmth of his skin settled her. Then he moved his hand downward to press across her ass. Her muscles clenched as she waited for him to raise and then drop his hand on her, but his intention wasn't to spank. He pressed down, causing the vibrations to pound between her legs more strongly.

"Just focus on this. Ignore the rest until you can focus on the rest."

She nodded, squirming and rubbing herself against the bench.

Then his hand came down on her. She jumped at first at the sensation, but then relaxed again. Instead of calling up memories of Lucas, it made her think of the 24/7 she'd lived in before the island. It had felt like *playing*, but she remembered their sessions. Her master had warmed her up, not just hitting for the sake of it, but gradually coaxing her body to reinterpret sensation according to his whims. It was the same as what Asher was doing.

He went through each of the spanking implements: the paddle, crop, and flogger. But not the cane. The cane sat untouched as he slowly brought her to the tolerance level he wanted her at.

"You have a higher pain threshold than I was led to believe. That fucking idiot," he muttered.

She knew he was speaking of Lucas. Lucas didn't warm her up. He'd just thrown pain for the sake of pain at her, randomly delivered at the highest intensity right off the bat. He'd had no reason to care about her experience or her body's ability to take the pain and turn it into something pleasurable. Her cunt had dripped from it anyway, much like it was doing right now.

As Asher brought the pain level up, he moved the power of the vibrations up as well. She no longer felt tethered to the table. No bonds could hold her right now. She was soaring. She bucked like a wild thing, one moment thrusting her ass up at him, her body begging for more of the pain that had started an opiate-like reaction in her brain. The next second she was pulling away, pushing her pelvis against the vibrations so she could come again and again. Each sensation was equally enticing, and she couldn't stop the fight to have them both.

The tears came in earnest then, a catharsis. Things she'd held onto and kept buried deep inside, places in her soul where Lucas had touched her, which she'd never been able to get clean. All she'd been able to do was repress, bury. Now it all flowed out of her. The blows Asher was landing weren't even hurting her; she was too deep in, her brain releasing too many pain-diluting chemicals. But it was permission to cry, to let it out in ways she hadn't given herself permission to until this moment. Asher was right. Somehow she knew the nightmares would go away. Maybe not forever, but each time he could, and most likely would, bring her back here to the dungeon to purge her demons.

A moment later the vibrations stopped. She thought he was finished with her, but then a sharp crack landed on her ass that made her scream and fight to catch her breath. She turned toward him, the fear back in her eyes, but Asher had already laid the cane back on the table.

"Just a taste of punishment, kitten. I don't want you to think all pain with me is good pain. I don't want to encourage misbehavior. If you want good pain, all you have to do is ask. Never misbehave for it. I promise I won't make punishment pleasurable."

Grace was offended he thought she'd be a brat. Didn't he understand how grateful she was to be in his care instead of Lucas's?

He ran his hand lightly over the welt the cane had left. "Now tilt your hips so I can get inside you."

He left her strapped to the spanking horse while he fucked her, his hands spanning her waist, making her feel somehow even more vulnerable. He didn't ask her questions or intrude upon her thoughts as she cried. He must have known the tears weren't something he needed to ask about. Not pain or hurt . . . relief. For once he let her have the private moment inside her own head.

She didn't come again, already spent from the spanking horse, and her master didn't ask her to. He just used her body for his release, no words passing between them. Looking on, a stranger might have thought she was being abused. Unless it was someone like her. Other subs would know; they'd understand a merging was taking place that went far deeper than tab A in slot B.

Grace hadn't thought she could feel more completely his or that she could love him any more for all he'd done for her, but she'd been wrong. Somehow with Asher, she didn't feel judged or wrong anymore. Her history was a bad dream and her present wasn't something she had to feel ashamed for.

After he'd had his fill of her, he unfastened the straps and carried her upstairs to the bedroom. She fell asleep in his arms almost the moment her head touched the pillow and didn't dream again that night.

TEN

A sher watched through the window of his study as Grace worked in the garden and chattered on his cell phone to her friend. His hand hesitated over the old-fashioned window latch while he considered opening it and calling out to her, but he decided to leave her to her chat.

She was doing remarkably well. She'd had a few more dreams of beatings from Lucas, and each time Asher had taken her to the dungeon to remold and reshape the things running around in his pet's brain.

The second time she'd had a dream, she didn't fight him or show fear when he took her downstairs. She seemed grateful and relieved for the catharsis. Each nightmare only strengthened their bond as she came to count on and depend on him more. The nightmares had been gone for weeks now, though he still whipped and fucked her regularly.

Darcy had faded to the background of his mind, her death a bad mistake and bad dream of his own. He still found himself comparing the two women, which only brought on fits of guilt. How could he allow his last pet to shrink even the slightest bit in his memory after what he'd done? It felt wrong to care for Grace so much, as if he was somehow cheating on Darcy.

No matter how long he'd lived on Eleu under its rules, a part of him would always frame things in the old vanilla way, with the old rules of how relationships were supposed to be done. In reality, he wouldn't have been cheating on Darcy even if he'd had both her and Grace at the same time. That idea made him feel worse, because somehow he knew Grace would have been the favorite. He pressed his fingertips against his temples to block out the thought.

He couldn't imagine the kind of bratty fits Darcy would have thrown to get his attention off Grace and back onto her. In this alternate reality, he imagined he would have sold Darcy to another man before he would have let her hurt Grace in any way. He would have ensured the new master was good and decent, but she still would have lost if it had come down to it. How could he let himself think this way?

Asher pulled the book out, and the dungeon door creaked open. Grace had come to trust he wouldn't use the bullwhip on her, though it seemed to confuse her more as to its purpose, since he'd said the cane was for punishment. The symbol of what a foolish decision could cost had become too much to look at.

The whip was the last piece of Darcy that had been left in the open. All of her things had been packed away a little at a time in the months following her death. Most of that time was still a blur as he'd spent the majority of it so drunk the gaps in his memory resembled Swiss cheese.

His hand trailed lightly over the leather. He still couldn't look very long at the blood on the tip. Every time he saw the weapon hanging on the wall, he thought of Darcy. At times, it took several minutes to get his mind on Grace. The person who was here. The one who actually needed him. The one he loved most even though it made him feel bad to compare. It also scared him. If losing Darcy like that had caused him to spiral so far downward, what would he do if anything ever happened to Grace?

He had to bury Darcy. For good. It was too much having her memory hanging over everything. At first he considered putting the bullwhip in the bottom of the toy box. But every time he went to get something, it would be there, poking its little snake-like body out at inopportune moments as he pawed through the other items in the trunk for a riding crop or paddle or nipple clamps.

No, it couldn't stay in any space that was meant for him and Grace. The possibility of throwing it out or burning it crossed his mind, but he didn't feel ready for that step. Instead, he stuffed it in the back of a hall closet—out of sight, out of mind.

Determined to not think about it anymore, he stopped by the kitchen, then went outside to meet Grace in the garden. She was so adorable he could eat her, and probably would a bit later. She was on her hands and knees on a quilt, digging in the garden. He was surprised by how good at it she was.

She'd taken the garden design books William brought her and created something that was nothing short of a work of art, with colorful patterns and designs more intricate than the patchwork quilt spread beneath her. She'd even taken into consideration how the garden would look at different times of the year. Though they didn't have full seasons, a few of the plants went through various changes. She'd managed to make the garden flourish even though there hadn't been as much rain and the crops weren't doing as well as most years.

She wore a fitted, cotton top with thin straps that were falling off her delicate shoulders. Her denim shorts had been specially made with a small hole in the back through which a butt plug with a tail could be, and had been, inserted.

A headband with kitty ears held her hair back away from her face. He didn't make her dress like a kitty anime girl all the time, but seeing her mildly humiliated did something to him. Asher kicked his sandals off and came to stand beside her. She leaned against his leg like she always did, and he stroked the back of her neck. Her limbs were so glowing and tanned it was hard to believe this was the same thin, pale woman he'd bought months before.

"Kitten, you need to drink something. You've been out in this heat too long." He handed her a glass of lemonade he'd brought from the kitchen.

"Thank you, Master."

He sat next to her while she drank, stroking her hair. "Lie down on your stomach," he said when she handed the empty glass back to him. Her eyes didn't even question anymore. Whatever he asked her to do, she just did it. And he never got tired of that lack of resistance. Her fear of him had largely disappeared, but her manner more than made up for the shift. Though she didn't live in an active state of terror, there was an air of fragility around her that he wanted to protect.

When she was stretched across the quilt, he opened a jar of shea butter she'd brought with her but had failed to put on. "Are we falling behind on moisturizing?"

"I'm sorry, Master." And she sounded it. The tiniest mistake, and he could practically hear the self-recrimination bumping around in her head. "I meant to, but I got distracted by the garden."

His eyes shifted to the cell phone lying on the blanket. "And maybe talking on the phone?"

Asher hadn't physically punished her with the cane yet. So far her minor infractions had resulted in writing lines or standing in the corner. Once he'd put a gag in her mouth with something foul tasting, but harmless, when she'd slipped and spoken a little too casually with him. It had been an effective punishment.

But he hadn't used the cane, which kept her on edge any time she did something wrong, wondering if this would be the infraction that brought the full reality of punishment on her.

"I'm not upset with you. I didn't give you a specific time to do it by," he said. "Still, I like your skin soft for me. You know the sun dries you out, and I don't like that."

"I'm sorry."

He started rubbing the shea butter over her legs and feet, and smiled when she let out a moan and squirmed. She'd be wet, of course. Any time he touched her, in even the most innocent way, her body responded, eager and ready to be fucked.

"Grace, I have something important to talk to you about."

She got very still, the combination of his tone and the use of her first name causing her to grow wary. There was no sense dragging it out. He might as well just say it.

"I'd like to brand you."

Her head snapped around as she twisted to face him, that scared, pleading look in her eyes. God, it was so wrong, but he missed that look. It might be time to move them into edge play. His cock hardened, and if he didn't want to actually talk the issue out, he would have fucked her right here.

"Please . . . Master, why? What did I do wrong to deserve . . .?"

He gently but firmly pressed her head back down so that she was lying on the blanket again and started rubbing the cream on her other leg. "It's not a punish-ment. I know I said I'd never leave permanent scars. This isn't something I'll make you do. I'll let you choose. But it would really please me if you did it."

She twisted so she could see him and bit her bottom lip. "I don't know if I can take it."

Asher laid her other leg down and started massaging the cream into one of her arms. "The type of branding we would use on you is called strike branding. It will hurt, but probably not as much as you think. We'll heat hot enough to kill the surface nerves but not enough to reach the deeper tissue. It's not a pain that will linger like a minor burn does. It'll be sore during the healing process, but it won't feel like a burn afterward. I'd hold you while the brander did it."

He finished with her other arm and shoulders, then closed up the cream and pulled a piece of paper from his pocket onto which he'd drawn his estate symbol. "This is the symbol on the front door. Each estate on the island has a different one. The symbol is sometimes branded into slaves so others know which house she belongs to." He wasn't sure if she'd been exposed to enough other slaves to have seen a brand before. They weren't all that common on the island. "A master only brands a slave if he intends never to sell her, because you get very little out of a girl that's been branded by another man's symbol. Do you understand what this means, Grace?"

"It's like a promise? That I'm always yours no matter what?"

He smiled. She understood. "I won't ever break a promise to you, kitten. Ordinarily I'd just do it, but I already told you I wouldn't leave permanent scars. So think about it. I can get you some reading material so you understand more about what will happen and what the healing process will be like—"

"I want to do what pleases you."

Asher pulled her up off the blanket and held her. "You're such a good girl."

Grace fidgeted in the back of the limo. Asher sat beside her in a crisp, white shirt with the first couple of buttons unbuttoned, jeans, and casual shoes that the islanders were fond of wearing. He seemed at ease; meanwhile, she was falling apart on the inside.

Why did I agree to do this?

From the moment he'd first mentioned branding, she'd loved the idea of it, but feared the reality. In theory, it felt like the strongest bit of protection he'd ever given her, the most firm oath that she would always be his, and she'd always be safe and cared for. But the reality of the pain involved had caused her to wake in cold sweats thinking of it.

Asher had believed it was nightmares of Lucas again, and Grace hadn't corrected his assumption. She was afraid if she did, he wouldn't make her go through with it. And she needed to. She needed to see his brand on her forever, as if that one carefully placed mark could erase all of Lucas's careless marks.

Each time she woke in terror over the branding, he took her to the dungeon. She let the flogger fall over her, cried out her fears, and allowed herself to be taken where her master wanted her to go. She felt guilty he didn't know the real reason for her upset, that he thought he was spanking her for a different reason, but she kept the truth inside.

In the weeks following his request, he'd stayed true to his word, giving her all the information she could need about the procedure and how it would all go down.

But even so, she knew a few pamphlets could never prepare her for the burn of the branding iron.

She remembered times when she'd had minor burns and how the pain lingered on and on, feeling like it would never let up. And though Asher had promised the burning sensation would only last a few seconds and then be over, she couldn't quite believe it. Logically, she knew what he said sounded right. Minor burns didn't kill the nerve and that's why it hurt so much. But a brand, done right, killed the nerve. Even with that knowledge, in her mind and dreams, the pain dragged on and on and there was no balm or soft words or flogger that could soothe it away.

"You can't be comfortable like that. Lie down on my lap."

She hadn't been especially comfortable, no. He had her in full kitty mode. She wore a black leather miniskirt that had been sewn with the special hole for the tail. The plug was lubed and seated firmly inside her ass, the black fluffy kitty tail flowing out from the skirt. Her breasts nearly spilled out of a leather bustier. Her legs were covered with fishnets, and dainty black ankle boots were on her feet. She'd never say it, but she liked dressing this way for him.

The skirt rode low on her hips, leaving an expanse of flesh exposed for the branding. Gooseflesh popped over her hip, as if that part of her skin was taking the opportunity to get its last taste of something as simple as a cool summer breeze.

Her hair flowed loose down her back, held off her face with her kitty ears. She wore black fingerless gloves and her long nails had been painted white to resemble claws.

Grace settled her head on his lap and he petted her long, golden tresses, trailing down her back and over her ass. He ran his fingers through the fur of the tail, tugging it a little. She moaned.

"Such a horny little kitty," he teased, dipping fingers between her legs.

She wanted to meow.

At first she'd been afraid he was going to have her do all sorts of weird stuff that wouldn't be sexy at all. This kitten thing of his was definitely a fetish. Something he liked a bit more than just average. He seemed to get off on making her a little more animal-like, having her drink milk out of a bowl on the floor and making her beg for his cream.

He still hadn't used physical punishment, and she was beginning to wonder if he ever would. He'd once put her in a pet crate like what one might take a large dog to the vet in. It was small and cramped for a human, and it freaked her out possibly as much as pain would have. But he hadn't kept her in there long.

Her fears over the branding were compounded by anxiety over being out. They didn't come to town often. Asher wasn't punishing her by keeping her at home; he'd noticed her discomfort. He noticed everything.

After the way Lucas had treated her, going out seemed like an ordeal fraught with peril. She never knew how to behave and was constantly afraid she'd do something wrong that could somehow get her removed from his care. Asher had assured her such things didn't happen on Eleu, but she still couldn't make the fears go away.

The limo rolled to a stop in front of a tall, granite-colored building. The building was fancy and rich, and even though Grace knew this was where the brander's office was, it was still impossible to believe. There really were no poor people on the island.

There was only the rich, and their help. But the help lived with the rich. There were restaurants with wait staff and stores and such, but these places were run by some of the families who were indigenous to the island. The same people who made the special salve. It was impossible to think of them as the poor of the island because they lived in the most intricately designed huts, such works of art that one could perhaps refer to them as bohemian, but never poor.

When you passed a native islander on the street, you never felt a sense of envy from them. These people spoke the language of the island's volcanoes and ridges and plants. They knew the island's weather and moods. If they thought the things the rich did were odd or immoral, they didn't say anything. They seemed to take it all in stride, sharing the island, but maintaining a separate culture that outsiders weren't welcome to participate in. So which group was the haves and which was the have-nots? It was impossible to say.

Grace looked back at the building and winced, imagining the brander as some hardcore sadist that got turned on by causing women high levels of pain, or maybe got turned on by leaving such permanent marks with full permission from their masters. She shook the thought away. Asher had promised he'd stay with her. He stepped out of the car and extended a hand to help her out.

She smoothed the miniskirt down. At least he'd brought her out during the day. It felt less scary to be in town in the bright sunlight, so unlike the dark basements and buildings Lucas had taken her to after dark. The skirt barely covered her ass, and she knew if she bent over at all, her bare, wet pussy would be on display for anyone who cared to take notice of it.

Her fingers trailed over the platinum collar, as if checking to see that it was still there. Asher attached a long, platinum chain to the collar and led her into the building.

There were a few other slaves in the lobby, most of them naked or wearing less than she was. Despite sticking out, Grace was comforted by more clothing. Still, it didn't stop the men from leering, whistling, and making cat noises at her. She kept her eyes down, so she didn't see what Asher was doing, but she suspected he glared at the men, because after a couple of seconds everyone fell silent and went back to what they were doing.

She let out a little breath when they were alone on the elevator. Asher pressed the button for the appropriate floor, then backed Grace into the corner behind him and slid his hand between her legs. She let out a mewl and rubbed her crotch against his hand. He chuckled at her wanton behavior and pointed to a camera overhead. She blushed but didn't stop rubbing on him.

The brander was on the fifteenth floor, but they stopped on three. The doors opened, and a man got on. Grace watched his shoes as he shuffled onto the elevator.

"Asher," the familiar voice said in that way men do when they recognize one another and nod.

That voice.

It slithered over her, leaving a dirty trail that no soap in the world could wash off. She felt her heart start to pound, the throbbing noise pulsing in her ears so loud it dwarfed the sound of Lucas.

She was glad to be in the corner with her master's broad body blocking her in, acting as a shield. Her white fingernails dug into his side, and she hoped he wouldn't be angry if she left nail prints. It took all her energy and concentration to make her breath go in and out.

"Lucas," Asher said between clenched teeth. His voice was tight, and Grace knew he wanted the other man on the elevator with them even less than she did.

"How is the little slut? Obedient? Pleasing? If you're having troubles with her, I can give you some pointers. She was always very afraid of me," Lucas said.

She pressed her forehead against Asher's back, the feel of his warm, broad body keeping her grounded. Without him there, she was sure she would drift away.

Asher took another step back. It pushed Grace flush against the metal corner. Instead of causing her to feel claustrophobic, it made her feel safer, more protected. All sides of her surrounded by metal and Asher Collins. The muscles in his back were poised like a big cat, as if he might sprout fangs and pounce on the other man at any moment.

"I don't need any pointers, thanks. I believe I've got the situation under control."

Grace could feel the tightly-coiled violence, how it waited like a living energy, ready to spring should Lucas make a move toward them.

"I only meant that I could help if you needed it. You don't want to let her get out of control and forget which of you is the master. It seems somewhat questionable to me. I mean, she's not even kneeling."

Asher jabbed at a button on the column. Number five lit up, and the cramped metal box lurched to a stop.

"I believe this is your floor, Lucas."

"My floor is twelve."

Asher moved into the other man's personal space, shoving him against the elevator wall. "Take. The. Stairs. I don't want you near Grace. Ever. Again. I bought her to rescue her from you. You shouldn't be allowed to own so much as a potted plant." He held the door open while the other man stumbled off.

Grace huddled in the corner, her eyes closed, the tears inching down her cheeks. She opened them a fraction of a second too soon and caught Lucas's dark stare as the doors slid shut.

Asher held her against his chest the rest of the way up, and the brief pause on twelve where no one got on and no one got off.

The doors opened on fifteen, and Asher led her down the dark green hallway to the last door on the right. Inside, they were greeted by a good-looking blond man with tattoos that banded around his throat and up and down his arms. He looked like a cross between a surfer and a biker, but it was obvious he was better off financially than the average member of either group.

The man took one look at Grace, then at Asher. "She looks terrified."

Asher shook his head. "It's not all about the branding. We ran into someone."

The brander looked at her again, and she had to turn her gaze away from that assessing stare that seemed able to divine too much about her life from her eyes.

Asher directed her to a pillow on the floor, and she obediently went to it and dropped to her knees, glancing around the room to take in her surroundings. She hadn't expected the environment in the brander's office to be so soothing. It was as if they were there to get her hair styled instead of put a permanent scar on her. Everything was just so . . . clean.

The men spoke in hushed tones a few feet away. Every now and then she heard her name. It occurred to her that Asher knew this man, that they were perhaps friends. The blond had a kindness to his eyes, much like her master, and Grace felt calmer.

"Are you ready, kitten?" Asher stood over her, pulling her out of her thoughts.

"Yes, Master."

"It'll be five seconds of pain, then it's over except for the soreness. You can handle that. And I'll hold you while John does it."

She nodded, not trusting her voice. Five seconds could be a very long time when the time was filled with pain.

They led her into another brightly lit room, and Asher handed a metal disk to the blond.

"This is nice," John remarked, admiring the estate symbol. "It'll make a clean design."

She watched as the branding iron was heated, everything matching the pamphlets she'd been given to study. As the iron grew hotter, so grew her trepidation over her choice.

"Normally, we chain them down for this, but I know you can hold her still."

Those words lodged in her stomach like a stone, making it impossible for her to move without her master's assistance.

"Put your arms around my waist, kitten, and hang on tight." When she'd obeyed, Asher wrapped one of his arms around her back, holding her steady against his body, and with the other he cradled the back of her head. "Just breathe, baby. It won't be as bad as you think, I promise."

John moved behind her with the heated metal. A moment later, the searing heat was in her skin, melding with her and sucking the breath from her lungs. She let out a wail and almost vomited at the smell of her own burning flesh. The smell triggered her self-preservation instincts, and if her master hadn't been holding her so tightly, she would have struggled. *Why did I say yes to this?* She squeezed her eyes tight, trying to breathe through the pain.

As if reading her mind, the blond said, "It won't get any worse, and in a few seconds it'll get better."

"Five . . . four . . . three . . . two . . . one . . ." Asher said, steady and strong. He held her tight while she cried. The blond took the metal away, and unbelievably the burning sensation was gone. The skin around the mark felt tight and sore. But it was a kind of pain she could handle. Asher released her and brushed the tears off her face. "You were a very good girl. Come to the mirror and see my mark."

He took her to the mirrored wall. Her breath caught when she saw his estate symbol on her hip. Somehow she hadn't believed it would happen. He really wasn't going to ever sell her. A small smile curved her mouth as she stared at the brand.

John was giving Asher instructions for care and information on healing time, but she couldn't tear her eyes away from the mark on her hip.

"Do you like it?" he whispered, brushing his lips against the shell of her ear.

"Yes, Master."

"I'm so happy you did it." He clicked the leash back around her collar and led her out of the office. They didn't run into Lucas again.

Something was unsettling Asher. It had bothered him for the week since the branding. Grace had stopped having nightmares.

It wasn't the fact they'd stopped, it was why they'd stopped. It didn't add up. He'd believed his pet's bad dreams were the lingering remnants of Lucas haunting her. But if that were the case, wouldn't the dreams only start back again stronger after their brief run-in with her former master in the elevator?

He wanted to test a theory, and he hoped he was wrong. Grace was in the garden. She didn't have a single pair of denim shorts without the hole for the tail, so she was sporting the kitty look. He slipped up behind her, careful not to startle her, and tugged the tail a little, pulling it loose from her ass and then pushing it back in. She dropped the garden trowel and let out a delicious whimper, going to her hands and knees, thrusting her ass up at him, begging for more contact.

He'd been surprised at what a dirty little anal slut she'd turned out to be. Once he'd shown her how pleasurable it could be when done right.

As much as he'd like to play with her, there was something he needed to know first. "Grace?"

She stopped wriggling immediately and turned to face him, sitting back on her knees now with her legs spread, the way he'd taught her to kneel for him.

"Yes, Master?"

"Do you remember the last round of bad dreams?"

She nodded, a wary expression on her face.

"What were they about? Don't even try to lie to me."

The way her eyes widened, he knew he'd caught her. Even if she didn't say the words, he knew. The only thing left was to determine what was to be done with her. Still, she tried to stall.

"What do you mean?"

"Kitten, you really don't want to go down the doe-eyed road with me. Tell me what they were about."

She looked down at the quilt, wringing her hands in her lap. "The branding," she whispered, almost inaudibly.

His jaw clenched. Beneath the anger was hurt that she'd undermine what they had with silent lies. "You allowed me to believe you were dreaming about Lucas. You know that's why I was taking you to the dungeon and flogging you. Why didn't you tell me what the dreams were really about? Why would you hide that part of yourself from me?"

She sniffled, and Asher wanted to backhand her. How dare she make a bid for mercy, playing on his feelings for her after she'd lied to him, knowing full well how she was misleading him.

"Well?"

"I . . . I'm sorry. I was afraid if you knew how scared I was about the branding, you wouldn't do it. You said it was my choice, and I thought if you knew about the dreams you'd think I wasn't sure and you'd change your mind or let me back out. I didn't want to be weak and back out."

He wasn't sure what he'd expected, but it hadn't been that. Could he really be mad at her when her subterfuge had been because she'd wanted to wear his brand so badly?

He sighed and she looked up.

"What are you going to do?"

He just looked at her. She knew what he was going to do, but he said it anyway to leave no doubt. "Physical punishment." The wind seemed to carry his words far out to sea. "There will be no lies between us, Grace, not even the unspoken kind. Wearing my collar and my brand means every part of you belongs to me, including what goes on in your head. Come with me."

He felt her shaking behind him as he led her into the study, pulled the book out, and guided her down the stone steps. He'd been aroused after the branding, the last time she'd been this scared. The moment they'd gotten home, he'd taken her to his room and proceeded to use every toy at his disposal on her hot little body.

He fully intended to repeat those actions today, but this time, he'd finally punish her first. In truth, he didn't like hitting for punishment. He much preferred to turn that kind of pain into an erotic torture that would make her beg him to take her deeper into it. And once he'd punished her, he'd move her into that space again.

She didn't have to be told to go to the cushion. She just went and knelt on the large, fluffy pillow, waiting for instruction. Asher set up the table with toys and instruments of pain, then he covered her eyes with a blindfold.

"Master, please, I'm sorry," she whispered, the tears spilling out from under the dark cloth.

"I know you are, kitten. But you still have to be punished. I told you this day was coming. When I'm finished with you today, you won't withhold anything from me. If you think I'm misreading your feelings on something, you'll take the opportunity to correct my assumption. You will not go about with secret thoughts and feelings and fears. There will be no doors closed to me that I want left opened. Do you understand me?"

"Yes, Master."

"Offer me your wrists."

She took a shuddering breath and held her arms in front of her. He took a length of rope and wrapped each of her wrists individually, then went to work, tying intricate knot work.

When he was finished, he pulled her to her feet. She didn't struggle, but stumbled a little as he tugged her forward. When he got her where he wanted her, he looped her tied wrists over a hook that extended down from the ceiling. The movement forced her to go up on her toes.

"I'll be right back," he growled in her ear, sending a shockwave of anxiety through her that he could almost smell.

He returned a few minutes later with a pair of heels from her closet. He slipped the shoes on her feet to make up the height difference. As much as he enjoyed watching her up on her toes, he wanted her standing solid and level for this.

She jumped when he cut her t-shirt and bra off with a pair of scissors. Then he removed the tail and slid the shorts down her legs. He stood back for a moment to admire her, naked except for the ropes binding her wrists, the blindfold, and the black and white heels on her delicate feet. Next, he retrieved a spreader bar from the toy chest and locked her ankles into it so her legs were spread wide.

"How scared are you, kitten?"

"Please . . ."

His hand landed solidly across her ass, leaving a loud smacking sound and a red imprint with the outline of his fingers. "I didn't ask you to beg. I asked you to tell me how scared you are right now."

"As scared as I was the day you took me."

His hand fell on her again. "What did we say about lying, Grace?"

"I . . . I'm not lying, Master."

"Perhaps not. But you're misremembering, at least. You were broken then. I don't believe you're that scared now. Do you trust me not to harm you?"

She only hesitated a moment before she nodded. "Yes, Master."

"Then it's not like that day, because you didn't have any certainty in my ultimate goodness to fall back on that day. I'm going to hurt you. But I'm not going to harm you. Why do I have to hurt you today?"

"Because I wasn't honest about my feelings. I let you believe things were happening in my head that weren't happening and kept secrets about what was really going on."

He stroked her flank. "Mmm-hmm. Do you know why that will get you hurt?"

She was still and quiet for a moment, and he knew the only response she had was something along the lines of "Because I said so." Wisely, she chose not to say it.

Asher sighed. "Because if I don't know what's going on in your head, I can't be a good owner. I need to know where you are at all times, physically and emotionally. If something has you scared or upset, I need to know about it. You knew I didn't know what was really going on, and you were experiencing distress I didn't know anything about. You may have had your reasons, but it should have been left to me to decide how to handle your fears over the branding."

He picked up the cane and brought it hard across her ass. He smiled as she shrieked and jumped, the tears flowing faster down her cheeks.

"Tell me you're sorry."

"I'm sorry Master."

"After each stroke of the cane, I want you to say: 'I'm sorry I lied, Master. Thank you for teaching me.' "

"How many?"

"Until I think the lesson has been driven home."

The welts he laid on her ass came down in beautiful, perfect lines. The music of her screams and the obediently repeated verbal offerings drove him into a frenzy. When he'd marked the whole of her ass, he moved down her legs, then took advantage of the spreader bar to give her a few sharp raps on the inside of each thigh. That elicited several pained howls.

Finally, when she was shaking so hard he knew it was only the hook and the heels that left her upright, he put the cane down and stepped back, admiring his work.

"Well, kitten, you survived your first physical punishment. If you behave like the good girl I know you can be, these types of visits to the dungeon will be rare."

Grace flinched as he ran his fingertips over the heated welts. Then he got down on his knees behind her and trailed his tongue over each of them, causing her to shiver. He fingered her wet slit and tongued her, lapping at the liquid dripping from her pussy. Before she could come, he stood and pressed himself against her back, his lips grazing her ear.

"If I let you down, are you going to be a good little whore for me?"

"Yes, Master." She let out a pained hiss as she pressed her ass against him.

He chuckled. "Already forgetting the welts I just left on you?"

"N-No, Master."

His hands came around to her front, kneading her breasts and tweaking her nipples into hard little points. Then came the nipple clamps. Her crying had stopped until he put the clamps on, then the sobbing came back. It seemed half was in response to sensory overload and half was in anticipation of what might be coming next.

He unlocked the cuffs and took the spreader bar away and removed her from the hook. "Go get on the spanking horse."

She whimpered at the order, but she went, too scared to defy him with so many cane welts lining her ass and no unmarked spaces left for him to hit. He hadn't bothered to untie her wrists yet. She struggled up onto the spanking horse, straddled it, and allowed her bound arms to fall over the top end of the bench.

He flipped the switch and smiled at the way she bucked against the vibrations, grinding her hot little cunt against the vinyl, trying to come.

"Pace yourself, kitten." He had no intention of letting her have a quick come and roll over to sleep. He intended to use her until dinnertime, which was still another hour away.

As she rocked and rubbed against the bench, Asher massaged lube into her ass, finger-fucking her tight hole. He wasn't sure which she liked more, having something in her ass or having her clit vibrated. After a few minutes of her lovely begging, he replaced his fingers with a narrow glass toy, working it in and out of her.

"Please . . ."

"Please, what?"

"Fuck my ass."

"You've got fresh welts, kitten. If I fuck you, my body pounding against them will hurt." Those words only made her wetter.

"Master, please."

He laughed. "Well, you can't say I wasn't trying to be merciful."

He stopped teasing, lubed his cock, and seated himself fully inside her. She whimpered and writhed as he started moving. Her head was turned to one side, and he watched the confused play of emotions across her face. The feeling of his fullness inside her ass, the pain of the welts being repeatedly bumped, the intense pleasure of the vibrations as each thrust pushed her thighs apart more and caused her clit to make harder contact with the padded bench.

"Come, kitten, and I'll empty inside you."

She let out a guttural moan and obeyed.

ELEVEN

Months passed, and Asher finally put Darcy behind him. She would always hold a piece of his heart, but she was his past. Grace had continued to flourish under his care. Her nightmares had ceased, and it didn't seem that her former master haunted her anymore.

After the day at the brander's office, He'd feared he'd lose his progress with her, but the brief and unsettling exchange hadn't managed to take away her overall feeling of safety.

He absentmindedly ruffled his pet's hair. She knelt on a pillow next to him in his study, wearing a bikini and tan-colored pants. She'd been lonely, so he'd invited her into the study with him while he took care of a few matters with his investment portfolio. Grace kept herself occupied, painting a little clay pot she'd made. She'd been lining her windowsills with them for weeks now. Their happy presence made her room seem even brighter and just a touch bohemian, as if she'd become a true islander.

The brand was almost fully healed, leaving behind a clean scar of his estate symbol. Asher stroked his mark, and she smiled at him.

This was the scene that was interrupted by a knock on the front door at four o'clock on a Tuesday afternoon. A few sharp words were exchanged down the hall by William and whoever had come calling. Moments later, footsteps pounded down the hall, and two island officials stood in the doorway. One flashed a badge and the other produced a document.

"Asher Collins, you're under arrest for the murder of Darcy McDonald."

Their words turned the room into a vacuum where no air seemed capable of penetrating. Grace dropped the pot she'd been so carefully painting, and it shattered on the hardwood floor.

"I'm sorry, Master."

"Forget it."

Her face fell. They both knew nothing would ever be done about her breaking the little pot. Whereas, before the words "you're under arrest" had pressed into the room, she would have been caned for the infraction, or at the very least made to write lines or stand in a corner for a couple of hours. There wasn't time for any of that now.

He didn't bother stalling. What was the point? The more worked up he got, the more upset and agitated Grace would become. He could at least go away with dignity. His chest tightened as he looked down at her. She was moments away from uncontrollable sobbing fits. The moisture had gathered around the corners of her eyes, threatening to launch the tsunami of grief.

They must have found Darcy's body. So much time had passed; he'd thought it was over. Ironic that the moment he found himself finally able to move on and bury the guilt, her body should surface. It was as if she were punishing him from beyond the grave for loving Grace. For replacing her.

He could almost hear her voice in his mind. *Wasn't your purpose to atone? Not move on and live happily ever after?*

He moved to the front of the desk. "I'd like to request that you set my slave free off the island. Send her to live with her friend."

"I'm afraid that's impossible under the circumstances," one of the uniformed men said. "According to the law, in a situation like this, the individual under arrest loses all human ownership privileges, and the slave reverts back to being the property of her former master." He looked down at the document he'd shown a moment ago. "That would be Lucas Stone. He's already been notified and has requested that she be returned to him."

Asher bet he'd been notified. He'd probably spent every waking hour since the elevator incident, searching for the body.

Grace crawled to him and latched around his leg like a small child intent on stopping his progress out the door. She let out a blood-curdling shriek and kept repeating the word, "No, no, no, no, no, no, no, no, no."

He would have ordered her to pipe down and show a bit of decorum but he couldn't have reached her even if he'd tried. She'd gone somewhere inside herself. The vocalizations surfaced from wherever she was, but if he spoke, he knew she wouldn't hear him. If it was possible, she seemed to be in worse shape than she'd been in the day he brought her home.

"You can't mean to give her back to him. Whatever you think I've done, that's not Grace's sin. She's an innocent in this. Stone abused her. He left scars on her. If you have any decency at all, you won't send her back there."

Asher wasn't stupid. He wasn't about to admit to killing Darcy. In the first place, it hadn't been his hand that had delivered the fatal blow. It didn't matter how responsible he knew he was, he wasn't about to say anything that sounded like a confession. Whether they had the body or not, he would hold his tongue until he had further information in case there was still a way out of this.

One of the officials wrapped a hand around Grace's arm and jerked her to her feet. "I'm sorry, Mr. Collins. The law is the law. And unfortunately we have no legislation protecting the general welfare of slaves short of not killing them." He gave Asher a dark look as if to say death was far worse than abuse.

She was still chanting, "No, no, no, no, no," like a crazy person. Asher couldn't say he blamed her. A similar chant had started inside his own head, only he'd managed to keep it inside. For now.

"Let me just have a few minutes to speak with her alone, to say goodbye."

The officials exchanged a glance and shrugged, seeing no harm in it. One of them seemed sorry to be returning her to a man who might have been hurting her. "Fifteen minutes. We'll be waiting for both of you by the front door."

As soon as they were alone Asher hauled back and slapped her. He needed Grace to be lucid and to get over whatever hysterical episode she was having. They didn't have time for it. Her hand shot up to her cheek and her eyes immediately cleared and went to his. Her lip trembled, but she didn't say anything. She just stood there, quiet and waiting, and at least seemingly in control of herself for the time being.

"We don't have a lot of time here. I need you to listen to me." He unlatched the window and pushed it open. "You have to leave right now. Go to the dock and use my boat. It's not meant for taking far out to sea. Just take it out about a mile and then circle to the other end of the island where the trees are denser. You'll see the huts that the natives live in. A friend of mine, James, lives with them. He's got blond hair and brown eyes. I want you to give yourself to him and do whatever he says. He'll protect you."

Asher pulled her against him, knowing he was probably crushing her, but she seemed too dazed to protest. He inhaled her coconut-scented shampoo. She smelled like the island. When she didn't immediately answer, he shook her.

"Do you understand me?"

"Yes, Master." Her voice was so small. He would have given anything to change things. Why the fuck hadn't he and James put the body in an incinerator like they had some sense? No body. No crime. But no, they'd stupidly buried it. Hadn't they watched enough television to know nothing ever stayed buried? Hadn't he known on some level that this would come back to bite him at the worst possible time? A part of him had wanted to get caught back then, but that line of self-destructive thinking had ended the moment Grace entered his life.

She reluctantly pulled out of his embrace and started to climb out the window, her movements stilted and robotic as if she were on autopilot. He was thankful the study was on the first floor. At least she wouldn't have to negotiate a high drop.

"Grace?"

She turned. The plea in her eyes startled him, as if she might beg him to run with her. But he couldn't. It was too risky. The officials wanted him more than they wanted her. He was the criminal in their eyes. She would only cost them reward money.

"You know I love you, right? I loved you from the first moment I saw you. If I never see you again, I needed you to know."

A tear slipped from the corner of her eye. "I love you too, Master. Maybe not from the beginning. I was too scared in the beginning."

"I know." He would always wonder when she'd started to fall in love, but he couldn't afford that kind of self-indulgence right now. Every minute they took talking was a minute she couldn't make her escape. He pulled her to him again, his mouth crushing hers, tasting her, probably for the last time. "Go," he whispered into her hair.

When she'd gone, he watched out the window as she ran to the pier. Every few minutes he glanced down at his watch. He could barely see the boat, a small speck on the water. He wondered if he'd even hear it start up. A few minutes later, he did hear it. From the study, it was a tiny sound, no louder than the buzz of a bumble-bee. Then the little white speck moved away, and he couldn't see it anymore.

Finally, he closed the window and latched it back. No sense giving the officials any help. He pulled the book out of the bookcase and was staring down the stairs five minutes later when the men knocked on the study door.

"Time's up."

"It's open," he said.

The door swung in, and the two uniformed officials stumbled into the room. "Where is she?"

Asher glanced up. If they bought that she'd escaped through some secret door or tunnel under the house, it would buy her a little more time to get farther around the island.

"She's gone," he said with a shrug.

One of the uniforms punched him in the jaw, and his head reeled back. He just laughed.

"We'll have you charged with helping her escape in addition to the murder charges."

"In the first place, I haven't murdered anyone," Asher said. "And in the second place, Grace is not a criminal."

"She's a runaway slave."

"She was merely following her master's orders. She wasn't breaking Eleu laws."

The official cuffed Asher using more force than necessary, then patted him down and led him outside while his partner took the bait and started down the dungeon steps in search of his pet. Idiots.

Grace stared at her master's house until it became an indiscernible dot on the horizon. She'd wanted to shout that he hadn't killed Darcy, but she'd been so panicked that every time she tried to make a word come out, the only one that would make it past her lips had been, *no.*

Thankfully, since Asher had slapped her, she'd snapped out of whatever that was and was at least able to focus on the task at hand.

She was far enough out now that she cut the engine and let the boat drift. A part of her was tempted to leave and never set foot on the island again. But it was far too dangerous. She had no idea where she was or what direction would take her back to the mainland. If she went the wrong way, the boat would run out of fuel and she'd be drifting out at sea, at the mercy of the elements.

Even if there was a chance, she couldn't bring herself to disobey his last order. She wiped her eyes with the back of her hand, sure her face was puffy from the tears. Not only was she convinced she wasn't fit to give herself to anybody in this state, she couldn't imagine being with someone besides Asher. Even if the order had come from him. It seemed profane.

The thought of betraying her master by letting any other man use her body made her stomach churn in rebellion. But she could barely bring herself to question the command. She'd do whatever he told her to do, even if it meant going to another man's bed.

The sun was setting when she reached the shore. A dense and foreboding jungle loomed in the distance, but on the coastline were the artistically thatched huts of the native people.

Torches were being lit, and fires were being stoked beneath the evening meal that had been hunted in the nearby jungle. Though some of the islanders owned shops and restaurants in the town and used money, a good portion of them preferred to live off the land as they had for centuries.

She was glad she was wearing something relatively normal. In her bikini and khaki cargo pants, she looked like a girl gone wild on spring break. But at least she didn't look like some kinked-out slave, except for the collar around her throat and the nearly healed brand on her hip.

As she neared the camp, a few of the islanders looked up. Their expressions weren't friendly. Maybe this hadn't been such a good idea after all.

She didn't see anyone fitting James's description. Maybe he no longer lived with them, or maybe there was another settlement on a different part of the island Asher wasn't aware of.

A few of the men moved away from the fire toward her. She had to fight every instinct not to run, but the only options this late were the jungle or the boat, and neither place seemed safe in the encroaching darkness.

They spoke rapidly to each other in their native tongue. Grace wouldn't have understood them even if she'd considered herself fluent. They were speaking far too fast. A few kept pointing to their throats, and she knew they were having some kind of conversation about her slave status.

"Do any of you speak English?"

They stopped for a moment and blinked at her. She didn't know as much about the politics and culture of the island as she'd thought. She'd lumped all islanders together as if they were one cohesive unit, not bothering to consider that different groups might live in different ways. These people were clearly not integrated with the main island like the shop owners were.

She started to back away. Angry natives and a language barrier didn't sound like a fun time. They advanced. Grace stumbled in the sand as she ran, and a moment later they surrounded her, talking fast and loud as before. She moved her hands defensively in front of her face. Without language, she had no means to talk herself out of the situation, nor did she know what might come next.

"Stop."

The men looked up and Grace turned in the direction of the clearly spoken English. The man had no accent as a native islander would. He looked like a surfer. His sandy blond hair, streaked with lighter gold from the sun, fell in a sexy mop over his eyes. She couldn't tell from just the torchlight if they were brown.

The surfer turned to the men and spoke in the island language, calmly and reasonably. The men looked back at her as if deep in thought, then back at the blond. Finally they spoke in what sounded like agreement and went back to the camp.

The man held out a hand to help her stand. "There's a price on your head, you know. All runaway slaves fetch a high reward if returned to the officials. They were arguing over what they should do with you. I said we should bring you to camp and find out your story before we make any rash moves. I'm James."

Words tumbled fast, before she could stop them and run back to the boat to form a Plan B. "I'm Grace. I belong to Asher Collins. He's been arrested for the murder of his last slave. He helped me escape so they wouldn't take me and said to come to you and give myself to you, that you'd keep me safe."

She'd taken a chill in the night breeze and wrapped her arms around her frame to ward it off, wishing she were wearing something warmer. James stared at her for a long time, long enough she feared he'd turn his back on her and leave her there in the dark. Finally, he started back toward the settlement.

"Come," he called quietly behind him.

She somehow made her feet move and followed him into the camp past several huts until he stopped at one and pulled back the heavy burlap that served as a door.

"Inside," he said.

She went in, but when she turned around, he was gone again. A few moments later, he returned with two plates of wild boar that must have been roasted over open flame all day. The boar was surrounded by rice, a few vegetables native to the island, and several rings of fresh pineapple.

"Sit."

She was confused by his sudden monosyllabic nature. He'd spoken in full sentences before she'd told him why she'd come. She sat on the rug and he gave her food. He put his plate on the ground and left again, returning with two cups of water.

She hesitated before she spoke, uncertain if he might punish her. But Asher said he'd keep her safe. That he was a friend. If her master trusted him, he must be okay. "Will you keep me?"

An endless stretch of silence hung between them, interrupted only by the sound of crude flatware scraping across plates. He ate several bites of the boar as if he hadn't heard her, as if he were lost in his own private world where no sound could penetrate. What would happen if he didn't want her?

As much as she couldn't stand the thought of giving herself to someone else, the reality was that Asher was gone and someone would have her now. It was better to belong to the man he'd chosen than to Lucas. She had to keep that thought in the front of her mind. Anyone was better than Lucas.

She was trying to gather the courage to speak again when he looked up at her, his face unreadable.

"Yes."

She let out a shaky breath and went back to her plate. He didn't speak again, didn't look at her, didn't try to touch her. It was then that she noticed the pain that seemed to surround him like a death shroud. She wanted to know what had driven him out of the fine mansion he must have once occupied to live with this tribe by the ocean. But she knew it wasn't her place to ask.

When their plates were clean, he still didn't make a move toward her. She wondered if he could feel her pain over losing Asher and if it added somehow to his own.

She'd always hated the saying "Misery loves company". Misery hated company; it only made the blanket of pain that much thicker and impossible to untangle oneself from.

He didn't seem committed to the idea of her being there, and the fear of what that meant hit her in the gut like a fist. She had to make him want her there.

She gingerly reached behind her to untie the strings of the bikini top. Then she stood and let the shorts fall, and the bikini bottoms with them. He looked up at her, his gaze both hungry and distant. But he didn't make a move.

Grace sat back down, feeling too much on display standing naked in front of him. He wanted her; it was in his eyes. All she had to do was make a move to secure her safety. Conflicting thoughts tumbled through her mind so loud it blocked out everything else.

I can't just betray Asher. It's not betrayal if he ordered it. James won't hurt me. If he would, I wouldn't have been sent here. If I don't do this, he might throw me out. I need to convince him he wants me here. He's my only hope of surviving now.

Several minutes passed before she made herself crawl over to him, the tears sliding down her face. *This is what Asher ordered. I have to do this. How can I even think about disobeying him in any way after everything he did for me?*

He tentatively reached out, his fingers feathering lightly over one breast before closing around it. The other hand threaded through her hair and wrapped around the back of her neck, pulling her to his mouth. The gesture was so much like Asher that she could close her eyes and it was him. So she did.

She was lost in the heady daydream of Asher holding her, kissing her, when she was pushed away and ripped from the fantasy. She looked up, afraid he knew she hadn't been with him as his lips had stroked over hers. Afraid he might punish her for it, and so conflicted over who she should be loyal to now. When her eyes met his, it was that same agonizing pain on his face.

"I'm sorry . . ." She hesitated, unable to let the word *Master* pass through her lips. Not yet. He would insist at some point, and she'd have to obey. But she wanted to hold onto the one remaining thing that tied her only to Asher for a little while longer.

"I killed Darcy," he said, his voice flat of emotion.

The admission had her scooting away. Did Asher know? He had to know. William said it was an accident—not by her master's hand. Accident or not, the knowledge that the man she was with had taken a life had her moving as far from James as she could get without leaving the hut.

"I won't hurt you."

She wanted to believe him.

Minutes crawled by and he sighed. "I can't do this."

Those words had her scrambling back to him, desperate to change his mind, knowing what would happen if he wouldn't keep her. "Please, I can't go back to Lucas. You don't know what he's like. Please don't send me away—"

"Get dressed."

She wanted to protest, but his decision had been made. He stood and gathered their dinner plates. Her hands shook as she fumbled with the bikini and pants, feeling stupid, exposed, ashamed, scared. So many feelings and no feelings all at once as a part of her seemed to numb out over the idea of being returned to the man she loathed and feared.

"I have to turn myself in. I can't let him lose another woman he loves because of me." James looked at her then, as if just now realizing she was in his hut, so lost in his own head he hadn't stopped to think how his previous words had sounded. He brushed her hair back from her face and wiped her tears, then pressed a kiss to her forehead. "Shhhh. I'll fix this. I promise."

Grace just stared as he crossed to the door flap and peered out.

"I want you to stay in this hut. I'm going to tell them you're mine and that I have to go do something but may send a friend for you. If anything happens and Asher can't come, if they think you're mine, they may let you stay."

Purpose attached itself to him, and he seemed to come alive as he packed a bag for his journey. "How did you get here?"

"Asher's boat."

"Good. I need to use it. I'll take it back to his house, then go into town from there."

She knew enough about the layout of the land to know going through the jungle would be far quicker, even on foot, than traveling around the circumference by sea. But going through the jungle was more dangerous, and alone, James faced better odds if he took the boat. She just hoped there was enough fuel to get him back.

He went to the door again and stopped. "When Asher comes for you, tell him his forgiveness means everything to me. I know he wouldn't have sent you here if he hadn't forgiven me. I've tried to forgive myself, but it's just not working. Maybe doing the right thing will fix that."

She sat by the door, listening as he explained things to the natives, then all was quiet outside the hut.

He'd only been gone a short while when one of the islanders that had first chased her came in. She swallowed around the lump in her throat as he brought her outside. Several men held torches and each had a small bag of provisions looped over one shoulder. Whatever James thought they'd agreed to, they obviously hadn't. They were yelling at her in that language she didn't understand. Then they were dragging her through the jungle toward the center of the island and the waiting bounty.

It was midnight when the officials returned her to Lucas. With the shortcut through the jungle, they'd beaten James to the prison. Money talked, even to natives living off the land. The trade had been fast, with the officials saying things in the native language she didn't understand, catching only the "thank you" part. Then they'd taken her back to Lucas, despite her pleas for asylum from him.

As she cowered in the dungeon, the only bright spot was the hope that James would make it, do the right thing, and then Asher would be freed to come after her. At least she had that hope to cling to. She knew she'd need it.

"Miss me, pet?" Lucas's cold, dark eyes were almost enough to make her start screaming and begging after only three minutes in his care. But she remained silent, mentally calculating in her head how close James was to the station, and how long it might take him to give his confession, and then how long it might take Asher to get free and come find her. She shuddered over the idea of all the extra time she'd have to wait as he made his way over to the natives, only to discover they'd returned her to the officials.

With all that, it would be morning before he could get to her. Surely she could hold out and not betray him until morning. A part of her knew Asher wouldn't blame mée

her for anything she submitted to in this dungeon. Still. She felt she should be strong for him and not capitulate too quickly. She wouldn't be able to live with the shame if she did.

He'd wanted her to go to James and submit for her own safety. He didn't expect her to hold out on his account. He wanted her safe and alive. She had to admit she preferred safe and alive as well, but safe was no longer an option with Lucas calling the shots.

"We've got a lot of bad training to undo," Lucas said. "When I saw you in the elevator, how completely you'd given yourself to Collins, I realized I gave up on you too soon. I should never have let you go."

"But you did."

His hand came across her face swift and sharp. "You filthy slut. It's only because I'm merciful that I'm keeping you for myself. I should whore you out." He ran a finger over the platinum collar, disgust in his eyes.

"You'll have to chop my head off to get it off," she said, unsure where her sudden bravery was coming from. All she knew was that she only had to endure a few hours with him, and she'd be damned if he broke her down to the terrified creature she'd been in that time. She didn't like the idea of Asher riding to the rescue only to see her submitting to her former master without much of a fight.

He laughed. "Oh, it's going to be fun breaking you back down. I thought if Asher killed his last slave, then surely he was a bigger bastard than me. But when I saw you with him in town that day, and you looked . . . happy . . . Well, it seems he had different intentions for you than I did. As to your collar, I'll call a locksmith in the morning. We'll have the offending object off your throat by lunchtime. I expect I'll only have to withhold meals for a couple of days and you'll be back to where you were before. Don't think you've suddenly gotten strong. You've just gotten spoiled. It's a very different thing."

Grace didn't comment. There was no sense baiting him more. If she pissed him off enough, he might lose control and kill her. It was obvious the little bit of sanity he had was becoming dangerously frayed. She was the one project he seemed determined to finish.

She closed her eyes, trying not to see the look that would be on Asher's face when he discovered her dead in Lucas's dungeon. To come this far, only to end like that seemed stupid at best. Whatever her captor managed to deal out to her in the next few hours, it would happen, and then it would be done. All she had to do was survive it.

She cringed when he stroked her collarbone. "Pity you'll lose this tan. I prefer you pale and vulnerable. I think I'll take great pleasure in watching the golden color drain from your skin day by day until you've paled out. You'll never see the sun again. I hope you enjoyed it while you were over at the Collins' Vacation Spa."

"Why do you even keep a slave if you can't take care of one? You know the value drops when you do that shit."

He shrugged. "You fetched a high-enough price. There is always someone willing to pay. Always someone with similar tastes and ideas of what a slave should be, but I won't sell you again. We are forever, Grace. I should have known the moment I laid eyes on you that you would be the one."

Having grown bored with the pleasantries, he pulled a knife from his pocket and cut the clothes off her. Tears sprang to her eyes when he yanked her hair back, turning her this way and that, inspecting his returned property.

He cursed when he turned her around, and she knew he'd seen the brand. At the time Asher had done it, it had felt like safety, a guarantee of some sort. But there were no guarantees on this island, and now all it did was anger the man she was currently with.

"You little cunt." He spun her back to face him, obviously unable to bear looking at Asher's estate symbol a second longer. Enraged, he grabbed her by the throat and pressed her against the wall. "You have the nerve to talk about devaluing property? Whatever made you think you had the right to wear his estate symbol? Did you really think you'd be free of me forever?"

What the fuck did he mean did she really think she'd be free of him? He'd *sold* her. He'd seemed thrilled to get rid of her because of that last piece he couldn't break or have, or whatever insane babbling he'd been doing the day of her sale. Back when he'd been so smug and convinced Asher would break her beyond recognition and finish a job he was either too lazy or incompetent to finish himself. Now he seemed motivated to try again.

"Answer me, slave."

"You sold me. So, yes, I thought we were done." She hadn't uttered the word *master* yet, and hoped somehow she would get out of here without ever having to refer to him in that way again, but somehow she doubted it. Rescue was still a long way off. *If it's even coming at all.*

Although she had some idea of how things were *supposed* to play out, it actually happening that way was still in the air. The boat could run out of fuel, and James could be stranded. He could change his mind, leaving Asher to pay for his crime. He could confess, and they might not believe him, or they might keep them both in custody, anyway. There was no guarantee her master would be released at all.

She shivered as that realization fully sank in. What if he never came for her? She'd torture herself forever wondering what had happened, each day her hope of rescue shrinking smaller and smaller. She pictured herself back where Lucas had her before, maybe worse. Because he was right. She *had* been at the *Collins' Vacation Spa*. She'd been living a life of luxury and pampering and love.

His hand squeezed tighter around her throat, cutting off her oxygen. "My, have we got our work cut out for us. After I get that ridiculous collar off your neck, I'm going to cut that branding mark off. Since you've already depreciated, I'm going to brand your other hip with *my* estate symbol."

"P . . . please . . ." She felt herself turning blue, the words barely having enough room and air supply to escape.

"Please? Please what? Who are you appealing to? I control everything. I control your right to food, water, sleep, oxygen. Who am I that I control so much?"

She shook her head, knowing the stubbornness was stupid. She was buying herself all of what? Five seconds? Because in the next few moments she'd either say what he wanted to hear, or pass out. And she was far too afraid of what he'd do to her while she was unconscious.

Her fingernails clawed at his hand. Lucas loosened his grip a little, and she took in all the oxygen she could get.

"The things I did to you while you were with me were mild compared to what I feel like doing right now. You will die in this room. It can be right now, or it can be twenty or thirty years from now, if you're lucky."

If there was no hope of Asher's return, Grace would dispute which option was the *lucky* one. She could envision herself driving him to such a rage he'd kill her and all this would be over. But the hope of being rescued and being happy again held her in check.

He hadn't removed his hand from her throat, subtly reminding her he held the power of her life in only one of his hands. "Trust me, pet, you don't want to piss me off anymore than I already am. The sooner you get over this bizarre pride or loyalty or whatever it is and submit to me, the better for you. Who am I?"

She looked into his cold, obsidian gaze. "You may get me to say the word, but know this, you will never truly own me. That right belongs to my real master. You might take his symbol off my hip, but there will always be a scar that reminds us both what was there. And you might take his collar off my throat, but you'll never erase his name from my soul."

A moment later his fist came back, and then she sank into blissful unconsciousness.

TWELVE

It was nearly sunrise when the official unlocked Asher's cell. He'd been having a nightmare of Grace crying out for him from Lucas's dungeon. In the dream, he'd been locked up, unable to do anything for her. Though awake, the dream clung to him like a memory of something real.

"You're free to go."

"What?" Maybe he was still dreaming. He couldn't have heard the man right. They'd questioned him for hours, saying they had the body so he may as well confess. The only thing he'd told them was that he hadn't killed Darcy. In his mind he apologized to her. Of course he knew he was still responsible for it. Darcy had been his responsibility, and she'd had no true power to fight his wishes.

Even if it had been James that landed the fatal blow, it was still his fault for not whipping her himself and for leaving her alone in the aftermath. But disclosing the full truth wasn't wise right now. Grace was out there, and he couldn't consign himself to a prison sentence, knowing what that might mean for her. There was no guarantee she'd made it to James.

He stood there, the cell door flung wide, while the guard raised an eyebrow.

"Well? Are you institutionalized after only a few hours? Get the fuck out. This isn't a hotel."

"I don't understand." *You idiot, don't ask questions, just leave.* And yet, he couldn't make himself move. It was too surreal. He'd thought it would be months before he got out and then it would only be if he was incredibly lucky and could somehow convince them he wasn't a killer. To be released before the sun rose was hard to process.

"It seems someone has materialized to take the rap for you. James LaFont. Name ring a bell?"

Asher just stared, unsure if admitting to a friendship with James would land him right back in the cell or if denying any knowledge of the man would just look more suspicious. James had confessed? So who was with Grace?

When Asher didn't say anything, the guard continued. "LaFont claims he took your slave off the property without your knowledge to borrow her and that in the course of the time at his home, there was an accident. He confirmed where the body was buried. According to his story, he couldn't bring himself to face you afterward and fled to the other side of the island to live with the natives."

At least the story meshed with him not saying anything one way or the other about knowing James. He finally made his feet move out of the cell and out of the station. He called his driver to bring the car. He wanted to talk to James, but he knew they wouldn't allow that right now, and he needed to get to his pet.

When he got home, William said James had been by and confirmed Grace was at the camp. In all likelihood, she was safe and sound with the natives. But what if she wasn't? He couldn't shake the dream of her crying for him in Lucas's dungeon.

Many crops were doing poorly this season. Hunting was probably a little rough, too. Which meant even those who lived off the land weren't immune to the promise of money and the comfort it could buy. If she was with the natives, safe and sound, she'd still be with them if he checked the Stone estate first. But if she was with Lucas, any second he wasted could end her life.

Grace's teeth clattered as the bucket of icy water splashed across her face, rousing her from unconsciousness. The water dripped down her body as she tossed her head back to get the hair out of her eyes. It took her a moment to figure out where she was, and she cringed when the Australian shepherd started licking water off her thigh.

"Not now, boy. I get first dibs, then you can play." He swatted the dog's haunches, sending him to the corner to sulk. "Morning, pet. Did you dream about me?"

"Unfortunately, yes."

He raised a hand as if to strike her but quickly pulled it back. "Oh no you don't. I know your game. You want me to either kill you or keep knocking you out. But if I do that, where's my fun?"

Grace pulled experimentally on the chains. Her arms ached. They were raised over her head, the shackles looped around a large, metal ceiling hook in the center of the dungeon, the kind of hook a pirate might use for a hand. Lucas had used a spreader bar to keep her legs extended so she couldn't kick out at him. The temptation to do so was powerful.

Now that she'd awakened, the idea of rescue seemed almost stupid. Even if James had good intentions, as soon as he'd gotten back to civilization, he would have rethought things. He would have realized some random slave he didn't know wasn't worth it. He would have justified leaving Asher in prison so he could have his own life. They obviously hadn't spoken for a long time, why should he give up everything now? He wouldn't. And he hadn't.

Either way, Asher probably said something incriminating during questioning. If that had happened, it was unlikely they'd let her master out.

The idea that she'd end up giving in to Lucas turned her now empty stomach. Asher had kept her so well fed that missing a single meal felt like cause for panic. The tears started to move down her cheeks.

"There she is," Lucas said, approvingly. "I knew you were in there somewhere. My frightened little mouse."

While she'd been unconscious, he'd set a table up with various whips he liked to use on her. He preferred things that marked well, broke the skin, left scars. It was as if he chose to mark her because he couldn't truly have her. It was the only way he could be assured his name would remain in her memory for any reason at all.

A wicked-looking knife gleamed from the table, the kind meant for skinning animals. It could take off thin layers so as not to waste lots of meat. Grace shuddered. He really intended to just cut Asher's mark right off her. The tears came harder.

Even if her master was coming for her, Lucas was ready to get started now. His sadism likely hadn't been fed in months. She knew she wasn't going to be rescued before he flayed the brand off her hip. He had a metal disk on the table with his estate symbol, as well as the tools needed to heat it.

She flinched when he brushed the hair out of her eyes, a false kindness that would evaporate as quickly as it had visited. The walls were closing in. She felt like the inmate about to be put to death, watching the red phone in the last few seconds, hoping for a reprieve. *Ring. Ring. Ring. Goddammit, Ring.*

But there was no phone and no reprieve coming. Instead, she cried out as the whip came down on her, tearing at her skin like a child ripping the wrapping off a gift. She felt the little drops going down her back that weren't water. Then she was suddenly numb, and she couldn't feel anything anymore.

Grace couldn't be sure of the amount of time that had passed since he'd started, but Lucas finally grew bored with whipping her. If the hook hadn't been holding her up, she would have fallen to the ground long ago.

Ring. Ring. Ring. Please ring. That bright red phone, still in her head, still standing there silent, mocking her. Refusing to give her freedom.

"Why couldn't you give me what you gave him? You little bitch. I brought you here. I'm your true master. How could you be such an ungrateful cunt that you wouldn't give me everything?"

She was crying too hard to answer him, and he seemed to be speaking more to himself than to her anyway, so she remained silent, hoping somehow to disappear and evaporate into a mist that could slide underneath the gap in the door and up the stairs to safety.

"You will give me everything. Do you understand me? Every fucking part of your soul will be mine. You'll belong to me so deeply you won't even remember his name." The whip came down across the center of her back, flaying another piece of her skin open as he unleashed his anger. The pain snapped back into sharper focus.

"Please," she whimpered.

He hadn't made her address him properly yet. But it was coming. She could feel it. He was waiting for the right moment to wring the word from her lips. And he would succeed, so much more easily than she'd ever wanted him to. It was already becoming clear how very little it would take to reduce her to the scared animal he'd turned her into. Asher may have dressed Grace up like a kitty, but it was Lucas who had truly made her an animal, and it was Lucas trying to return her to that state now.

He placed the whip on the table and moved in front of her, hooking his hand around the back of her neck and pulling her to him. His mouth crushed hers, his tongue sliding inside her like a serpent. She tried to pull away, but there was nowhere to go.

"Well, if you don't want to kiss me like you mean it, maybe we should go ahead and start with the fun stuff."

Her eyes went to the knife and branding tools. "N-no. Please."

"Please what? Say it, and I might spare you a little longer. He's not coming for you. He's in prison. He's never leaving prison, and you're never leaving this dungeon. So tell me, pet . . . who am I to you?"

The devil. But she'd already lost the courage to say it out loud, so she stayed quiet.

He grabbed her hair and pulled, wrenching her head back, and then he pressed the knife to her throat. "Or maybe I should just skin you and be done with it. What do you think? Are you worth the effort and cost to keep alive?"

Her heart was fluttering in her chest so fast she couldn't think. Then the dog started barking. Lucas never let him see this part. She looked over at the Australian shepherd. He'd been getting more and more agitated as things went on, and now it seemed he was aware a life might be on the line, and he didn't like it, either.

Lucas sighed loudly and went over to the door, flinging it open. "Outside, Jack."

The dog looked between them, shifting from barking to growling.

"Now!"

Jack glanced warily up at Lucas and then darted from the room, his tail between his legs. Lucas slammed the door. "Stupid dog. Papers or no papers, he behaves like a mutt."

Then his attention was back on Grace. He took a scrap of black fabric from the table and blindfolded her. She jerked in her bonds as he ran the flat of the knife along her cheek. "Come on, pet, who am I? Tell me, and I'll fuck you before I brand you. It'll buy you some time, yeah?"

She stood, shaking in the chains, the chill coming back. He'd juxtaposed the worst two suggestions he could have given her: raping her, or cutting the brand off and putting his own mark on her. Either way, it was all going to happen. The only thing that made a difference was the order. She'd hate herself if she betrayed Asher this soon when at most she'd get an hour's reprieve. Maybe not even that, since Lucas seemed so excited about the branding concept.

"Fuck you."

She heard him put the knife back on the table and then he wrapped a hand around her throat. "Say it, you bitch. Say it, or so help me, I will choke the life right out of you."

He was already doing it: choking her. She was helpless to fight him, without even free hands to claw at him this time. He was so lost in rage, Grace wasn't sure if he was aware of the fact that she couldn't say anything in her current state. She felt herself about to slip into unconsciousness again when the door banged open and she heard a crack like the sound of thunder in the air.

Immediately the pressure released from her throat.

"Get your hands off my property."

It was the red phone.

"Master!"

"Take the blindfold off and step away from her."

Lucas seemed to hesitate, and then that loud thunder sound happened again. That got his fingers moving. "How did you get in here?" he asked as he untied the scrap of fabric.

"It seems your servants don't like you anymore than anybody else on this island. It also seems that they fully support the idea of me killing you, since, if no one talks, they get to live off your wealth indefinitely."

Grace blinked as the blindfold came off. Asher stood just inside the doorway with the bullwhip in his hand. The one that had hung in the other dungeon, that he'd said he'd never use on her. Lucas grabbed the knife, but before he could move toward Asher, her master flicked his wrist and the bullwhip snapped down on Lucas's hand, causing him to drop the knife and scream.

"Kick it over," Asher said.

"Fuck you."

"I don't swing that way. Kick it over."

When he hesitated, Asher let the whip go again. This time it hit Lucas's inner thigh, inches from his privates. Lucas howled and kicked the knife over.

"Good boy. And, just so you know, I could have hit the mark if I'd wanted to. I practiced and practiced with this thing, but I could never bring myself to try it out on a woman. Maybe this was what my practice was building up to. You think?"

Lucas grabbed his own whip off the table. Not nearly as impressive as the one Asher held.

Her master chuckled. "Mine's bigger than yours. I'll bet that's true on multiple subjects."

Grace wished she could enjoy this as much as he obviously was, but she was too scared that Lucas, weasel that he was, would somehow get the upper hand, kill her master, and then the plans for her would resume, making the rescue attempt barely a blip on the radar.

"P-please . . ." She couldn't get a full thought out, her lips were trembling so hard.

Asher turned toward her. "I'm sorry, kitten. I'll make it quick, and then we'll go."

Lucas rushed him while his attention was on Grace, and for a second the rotation of the earth stopped, the universe pausing entirely. But Lucas was so outclassed, his attempt would have been comical if she wasn't still chained and helpless. Asher hauled back and punched him hard in the face, and the earth was moving again.

"You stupid motherfucker." He beat on him for a few minutes with his bare hands until Lucas dropped the whip. "Grace, shut your eyes."

She didn't want to, but she knew he wanted to spare her the gore. She closed her eyes and listened to the crack of the whip and Lucas's screams until they both stopped and there was silence.

"Keep them closed. This is messy, kitten."

"Is he . . .?"

"Oh, yes. Like a doornail."

She heard the water of the sink as he washed his hands. Then he came back and unlocked the chains from her wrists and the spreader bar from her ankles, inspecting them and running his fingers over the raw areas.

His jaw clenched when he saw her back. "Baby, this is bad. I'd like to resurrect him just to kill him again." He took off his coat and wrapped it around her.

Grace was startled by sounds in the doorway. She opened her eyes and looked up to see servants with dark smiles etched across their faces, all too happy to help dispose of the evidence. A couple of the men had saws to cut the body up, and a matronly older woman held a bucket with hot water, sponges, and bleach. Asher had obviously given orders on his way downstairs to rescue her. He hadn't been kidding about their disgust with the master of the house.

The woman set the bucket by the door and held a hand out to Grace. "I'll make her some tea while you take care of the body."

Grace looked up at Asher, careful to avoid the mess on the floor.

"Go on. I don't want you down here while we finish."

She followed the woman up the stairs, clutching Asher's long coat around her body, feeling awkward that the woman had known the whole time she'd been with Lucas. But what could she do? The officials wouldn't have stopped him, and it might have put her own safety in danger. It occurred to Grace that, once on the island, there wasn't a huge difference between household servants and slaves. Maybe they'd become just as enslaved, depending on the goodwill of their employers for their safety and survival.

The tea was already brewing on the stove, and the woman poured some into two cups and sat at the table. She put a hand over Grace's. "It'll be over soon."

The woman looked tired, as if she'd seen far too much cruelty, even from the fringes. She looked as if she'd been through war.

"I was his nanny when he was a baby, long before we came to this place. He was always so spoiled, but I never dreamed he'd become this." Her eyes were full of sadness and guilt.

Grace drank the warm brew down, wishing they would hurry with the disposal. "Why didn't the others help me or those before me?"

"Lots of justification and fear in this house. And Lucas kept us all away. We didn't know details. It was easier that way to convince ourselves it wasn't that bad, or that somehow it was consensual. He was the worst with you, I think."

A little while later, Asher and the men came upstairs.

"Well?" the woman said.

"Incinerated. You can go take care of the clean up now."

The ride home was quiet. Asher held her in his arms, stroking her hair, careful not to put any pressure on her back. He mostly thought. About Darcy. About Grace. About the whip he'd killed Lucas with. He'd finally been able to incinerate it, after he'd used it for something good.

"What if you get caught and go to prison?"

"That won't happen. No body. No crime. And believe me, those three have so much guilt for not helping you sooner, they won't say a thing. Plus they helped dispose of the evidence, and they have that nice, big house to live in without an asshole bossing them around all day."

"But what if it does . . . happen?"

He sighed. Of course she'd worry about this. It was natural after what she'd experienced. "It won't. But in the extremely unlikely event that it did, my wishes for what to do with you would be honored. Because it's not a murder of a slave, it doesn't invalidate my right to ownership. You wouldn't be resold. You could either stay in the house with William and be free or leave the island. We can draw up paperwork indicating what's to be done with you if something ever happens to me."

"Okay."

When they got home, he ran a warm bath and settled her in it. He winced as he watched her fight the pain to sit in the tub. He'd seen the last marks Lucas had put on her, but only after they'd had time to start healing and closing. Fresh like this, they were almost enough to empty his stomach.

"This is going to sting, but I'll be as careful and quick as I can, all right?"

She nodded and gripped the edges of the tub. The water was already turning pink.

"How do you feel about what I did today?" He worried after witnessing that kind of violence from him—even with her eyes closed—it would change how she saw him. He didn't want to become another monster in her mind.

"Happy. Safe," she said, leaning her forehead against the rim. She hissed as he cleaned around a particularly nasty area.

"I'm sorry, kitten. I don't want it to get infected. I should take you to the hospital."

"Please . . . no hospitals."

"It depends on how well this heals. If there is even the slightest sign of infection, I'm taking you in." He cleaned her wounds as carefully as he could, helped her out of the tub, and then patted her back with the towel.

She sat quietly, only flinching every now and then as he rubbed salve into the torn skin.

"You know, it's okay to cry."

"I don't want to cry anymore."

"Then you don't have to." He taped the bandages to her and took her to the kitchen and made her some scrambled eggs and juice. He'd asked William to keep a distance for a few days to let her get settled.

Asher watched her watching cartoons on the kitchen television while she ate. If he hadn't listened to his instincts and gone first to Lucas's estate, she could have been dead. He'd seen the skinning knife and branding supplies on the table. He gripped the end of the counter. If he'd arrived just a few minutes later, that bastard could have left his own mark, and Asher wouldn't have had the stomach to skin it off her. Things could have been so much worse.

When she was finished, he took her plate and rinsed it in the sink. "Would you like to take a nap with me? I'm tired."

She nodded, and he took her hand and led her upstairs.

Once in bed, Grace snuggled against his chest. "I love you, master."

"I love you too, kitten. Get some sleep. There's nothing left to haunt us now."

His words had fallen on deaf ears because her breathing had deepened. She was already asleep.